This book is dedicated to my family and the
Chickasaw People,
who are the unconquered and unconquerable.

DISCLAIMER

Although based on historical data, this is a work of fiction. Names, characters, places, and incidents either are the product of the author's imagination or are used fictitiously, and any resemblance to actual persons, living or dead, business establishments, events, or locales is entirely coincidental. All material in this book, including logos, text, and story are subject to copyright laws and may not be reproduced in any way without the written permission of the author, except in the case of brief excerpts in critical reviews and articles.

Author's photograph by:
Miko Hughes

Front cover models:
Eddie and Christina Jimenez

Cover design by:
Chris Ackerman/Signify Designs

Editing and interior formatting by:
Jenny Margotta

FIRST EDITION
2016

ISBN 13: 978-1535239721   ISBN 10:1535239727

GLOSSARY

Ababinnili: (Abaabinni'li') n., God in Heaven

Bois d' Arc: (boy-dark) n., a hardwood tree also known as Osage orange. Chickasaws used this wood to make hunting bows.

Chickasaw: (Chi-kash-sha) n., North American Indian tribe indigenous to the southeastern United States woodlands.

Chock: (cha-lk) n., a drink containing alcohol.

Chokma: (chook-mah) adj., good.

Five Civilized Tribes: Chickasaw, Choctaw, Cherokee, Creek and Seminole.

Hatuk: (hah-tuk) n., man.

Iskunosi: (iss-kun-oh-se) adj., little.

Koi: (Kohh-e) n., cat/feline.

Loksi: (loksi') n., turtle/terrapin.

Nashoba: (nah-shoh-bah) n. wolf.

Okla Chuka: (oh-kla) n., people; (chock-ah) n., home.

Osi llefenachi: Osi (Ohn-se) n., eagle; llefenachi (il-e-fe-nah-che) adj., proud.

Pashofa: (pah-shoh-fah) n., A traditional Chickasaw food consisting of cracked corn and fresh pork.

Tishomingo: (tish-a-minko) n., a town named after the last Great War Chief of the Chickasaws.

Toby: (toh-be) adj. white.

Willow flower: n., A willow branch carved into a flower. Chickasaw men gave them to the girl they wanted to court.

Yalhki: (yalhki') n., feces.

RETURN TO OKLA CHUKA

Mary Ruth Hughes

Mary Ruth Hughes

NORTH

Pontotoc County

Pickens County

Tishomingo County

Washita River

Okla Chuka

Tishomingo

Greasy Bend Inn

Nance Ranch

Lookout Mound

Panola County

Ardmore

CHICKASAW NATION 1896

Prologue

January 1899—Outskirts of Chicago

Osi stared out the train car window, vividly remembering the Cook County jail. The smell of human sweat, rotting food, and putrid drinking water were forever burnt into his memory. Now, however, he anticipated the taste of the crystal clear water rushing along Pennington Creek in Indian Territory. There was an old Chickasaw saying: *"When you drink from Pennington Creek, your soul won't rest until you return."* A smile flitted across his face; he was putting Chicago behind him and going home to Tishomingo.

The Pullman car was divided into two sections. He and Koi were in one compartment and the rest of the family occupied the other portion. Koi was sound asleep on the pull-down bed, but as Osi watched, she stirred then moaned. He steadied himself in the swaying train car as he went to check on her. When he was satisfied she was fine, he took his seat near the window and continued his thoughts.

The last few months seemed an eternity. He yearned for home, missing the tranquility of a peaceful life in the Chickasaw Nation. The Territory was going through major transitions with talk of Oklahoma becoming a state, but it seemed trivial compared to what he had been through the last two years.

Osi's thoughts were drawn back to the day Neville Cooper had arrived in the Territory.

◊◊◊

Osi remembered that day so clearly. Koi had recently returned home from St. Louis after attending school to study art and music. He and Koi were standing on the porch when Koi spotted her father, John Pritchett, and a stranger riding up to the house.

The stranger turned out to be Neville Cooper. John had overheard him complaining about the accommodations at the local hotel and had offered to let him come to his home for the night.

◊◊◊

Neville had arrived in Indian Territory in the summer of 1896. He was an attorney who had taken a position as an independent contractor, working for the federal government to assign roll numbers to the Indians of the Five Civilized Tribes. This proved to be ruefully deceptive.

From the moment Osi set eyes on Neville, he had feared this man could not be trusted, and his apprehension was not unwarranted. Osi shivered as he remembered the powerless feeling he had experienced when he thought he had lost Koi forever.

On her deathbed Koi's mother had tricked her into promising to marry the lawyer. But before Koi and Neville's wedding, Osi's mother performed a sacred Chickasaw ceremony, uniting them. That night they promised to love each other forever.

Osi was elected Governor of the Chickasaw Nation, but before he could be sworn into office, the vote was overturned by a recount. Luther Jackson, a progressive party member, became governor. Luther's liberal views were what the federal government needed in order to push for apportionment. Osi suspected corruption during the recount, but he didn't argue the point.

Amos Brooks, an old squaw man, found incriminating paperwork proving a sinister cartel worked in the Territory. According to these papers, Neville was in the thick of the schemes, along with Francis Kirby, the banker.

Osi traveled to Washington, D.C., where he delivered the

incriminating papers in person. That was all that was needed to bring about an investigation by the Commissioner of Indian Affairs.

On the way back to Tishomingo, Osi had gone to Chicago to confront Neville, who had taken up residency there soon after his marriage to Koi. Several months had passed and Osi wanted to know why Neville had chosen to stay in Chicago and not return to the Territory. A confrontation occurred, and during the scuffle, Neville was shot and killed and Osi was arrested.

Upon receiving a telegram with news of Osi's arrest, his family immediately traveled to Chicago to support him during his trial.

Osi was innocent, but convincing a jury of twelve white men seemed impossible. Luckily, the defense lawyer was brilliant. He demonstrated to the jury how the trajectory of the bullet made it impossible for Osi to have committed the crime. Then Neville's secret lover, Claire Dubois, took the stand and testified that Neville shot himself. These two testimonies were all it took for the jury to acquit Osi and he was released from jail.

◊◊◊

Osi's attention returned to the quiet Pullman car and he sat silently, watching Koi sleep peacefully in her bunk. He was comforted by the fact that she was now with him, and they were going to Okla Chuka.

His mind dashed from one vision to another, and he couldn't sleep. Just last night Koi had revealed that Kash was his son, not Neville Cooper's. He paused his racing thoughts, giving thanks to Ababinnili, the Great Creator, for all his blessings. He remained transfixed in prayer until he heard Koi stir.

"Osi?" Koi murmured.

"Yes, Koi," he said, going to her. "I am here."

"I dreamed you were still locked away in jail."

"I am here," he whispered again, hoisting himself up and under the covers next to her. He kissed her gently on the lips and stroked her long auburn hair to comfort her. He slid one hand down the center of her back until he reached the curve of her buttocks. With the other hand, he reached up and caressed her firm breasts. He could feel the hardness of her nipples. Excitement and anticipation overwhelmed them both. Their hearts pounded together in rhythm like the hypnotic beat of a ceremonial drum. Reaching the pinnacle of satisfaction, all earthly thoughts drifted into oblivion.

They lay side by side after their lovemaking, Osi cradling Koi in his arms until she went back to sleep. Wide awake, he basked in this blissful moment and knew he never wanted to let it go. A gratifying smile crossed his lips.

They were going home.

Chapter One

Ardmore

Late in the afternoon on a cold January day, the train screeched to a stop amid clouds of steam at the Ardmore, Indian Territory, railway depot.

Osi looked out the Pullman car window to see Ples, one of the Pritchetts' hired help, bundled up and perched in the driver's seat of the largest buggy owned by the family. Osi had expected him to be there, since Koi's father had sent Ples a telegram notifying him of their arrival time.

When the weary travelers stepped out of the train car, a gust of wind hit Koi and Kash in their faces. "Oh, my goodness, it's as windy and cold as Chicago," Koi remarked, readjusting baby Kash's knitted cap.

"So glad all y'all are home safe and sound," Ples said as he walked up to help with the luggage. "Mista Nance, I's so proud they didn't keep you in jail. Lots has been happenin' around here while y'all've been gone."

Osi acknowledged Ples with a nod while lifting Koi's heavy trunk onto the back of the buggy. "Let's get this luggage loaded then you can tell us all the news when we get settled in at Marietta Place. We'll be staying there a few days before going to Tishomingo," he said.

"And please be careful with the perambulator," Koi said. "I don't want it damaged. It's my pride and joy. Father purchased it while we were in Chicago."

After all the luggage had been loaded, and the five travelers were seated in the spacious buggy, Ples drove the

5

tired family along Ardmore's main street to Marietta Place, Gentle Woman's home on the far side of town. The name had been given to the property before Osi had purchased it for his mother.

"A nice bed sure will be comforting," John Pritchett said when they approached the house.

The little white cottage, a far cry from the tall buildings and the hustle and bustle of Chicago, looked particularly inviting, even in the cold dusk.

"It feels good to be back in the Territory," Gentle Woman sighed.

"I'll agree to that," John acknowledged.

Ples pulled the horses to a stop in front of the house and John helped the women down from the buggy. He escorted them inside while Ples and Osi unloaded the luggage and took the horses to the stable to bed them down for the night.

"Rose, I want you to put clean sheets on the beds. Everyone is looking forward to a good night's sleep," Gentle Woman said, tying on her apron. "I'll make us a meal." She went to the cellar and loaded a few jars of canned vegetables and peaches into her apron.

When she walked back into the house, Koi was coming out of the guest bedroom after putting Kash down for a nap. "What would you like for me to do?"

"Why don't you go out to the smokehouse and bring in a slab of bacon? Then go down to the cellar and bring up a few potatoes to fry."

"That sounds good to me," Koi agreed as she walked out the back door. "I'm hungry for a good home-cooked meal."

John and Osi sat in the parlor, having an afternoon smoke after bringing the luggage into the house. "I wonder what Ples meant when he said lots has happened while we were gone?" Osi mused.

"No telling. Nothing stands still around here."

Both men looked up when they heard a knock on the back door. Then they heard Gentle Woman say, "Come on in, Ples, the men are in the parlor."

"Have a seat." John said when he saw Ples in the doorway. "What's that news you were talking about?"

"Well, Mista Prichett. That banker, Kirby, got hisself kilt."

"What? When did this happen?" Osi asked.

"They found him several days ago on the road between here and Tishomingo."

"Who found him?"

"Some travelers," Ples answered. "The deputy marshal arrested Amos Brooks. He's sittin' in the jailhouse right now."

"Wonder why they arrested Amos?"

"Mista Prichett, I heared people talkin' and sayin' that Amos Brooks was the most likely person to have kilt him 'cause that banker's been loanin' him money and Amos don't have money to pay him back."

"Amos isn't the only one to have a reason to kill him," Osi said. "There's plenty of Mississippi Choctaws that have a bone to pick with him for making them sign over their future allotments. Hopefully, it won't be too long before the federal investigators arrive. Maybe they can get to the bottom of this thieving racket. The papers I took to the Commissioner of Indian Affairs are liable to incriminate a lot of people. Francis Kirby was probably trying to get out of town before they get here."

John took a puff from his pipe and blew the smoke into rings while voicing his opinion. "Looks like we've got our work cut out for us. We need to get over to the jail in the morning and see what we can do to help Amos. I'm eager to find out what he has to say about this."

Just then Gentle Woman called from the kitchen. "Y'all better get cleaned up. Supper will be ready before long,"

Ardmore Jail

When John and Osi arrived at the jailhouse the next morning, they found Amos asleep on a filthy straw mat in one corner of the fortified room that served as a jail cell. He was a pathetic-looking soul. His hair was caked with dirt and matted with lice nits and he looked and smelled as though he hadn't bathed in weeks.

Osi held his breath, bent down next to him, and gently patted his shoulder. "Amos, we've come to help you."

Amos startled awake and appeared confused before he spoke. "You two are a sight for sore eyes," he finally murmured as he struggled to his feet. "When are you gonna to get me outta here?"

"As soon as we can," John replied.

Grabbing Osi's arm, a terrified Amos said, "You knowed I didn't kill Francis Kirby."

"Yes, we know you didn't, and we're going to do our best to find out who did. Is there anything you can tell us about Kirby that we don't know?"

"Well, I knowed that he was up to somethin', and I don't think it was nothin' good. I saw some strange lookin' men go inta the bank the day before he was found dead."

John tried to reassure Amos. "We're going to do all we can to get you out of here."

"Don't let' em take me to Fort Smith and be hanged by Judge Parker!" Amos begged.

"You won't be going to Fort Smith. And Judge Parker's dead, so don't worry. But we need to leave you now to try to find the real murderer."

Osi stepped to the locked entry. He wanted out. It was a stark reminder of the days he'd spent in the Cook County jail. He never wanted to see the inside of another pit of putrefaction again.

On the ride back to Marietta Place, Osi was the first to speak. "I sure hope we can find the murderer soon and get Amos out of jail. The law was too quick to arrest him. It's as though they were looking for someone to pin the murder on."

"You know, I never cared much for that deputy marshal. I've got a sneaking suspicion that he might be involved. Wouldn't it be something if he did it?"

"Nothing would surprise me about this whole mess," Osi

replied.

Marietta Place

Koi walked into the parlor, bouncing Kash on her hip. "I was going to take Kash for a ride in the perambulator today, but I think I'll go see Jennie's new baby instead. I'm itching to see him."

Gentle Woman laid her mending aside. "I think you should leave Kash here with me and Rose while you go. There's a chill in the air, and I think he needs to stay inside."

"Okay. I shouldn't be too long. I'll get Ples to hitch up your small buggy, if you don't mind me using it."

"Of course you may take it, daughter. It'll be good for you to visit your friend. Go now, while you have the chance, because John will be wanting to get to Tishomingo right away."

Jennie's House

Koi drove across town to Jennie and her husband, Matthew's, house. She threw the reins over the hitching post and ran up the steps to the front door. She only knocked twice before the door swung open.

"Koi! I'm so glad to see you!" Jennie greeted her with excitement. "When did you get back from Chicago?"

"We arrived yesterday. I can hardly wait to see your baby. Your father-in-law announced his birth at Osi's celebratory dinner in Chicago."

"We sure missed Michael while he was gone. Matthew has been swamped at the law office. He mentioned the other day that he needed his father's advice before he could proceed with some pending law work."

"He should be arriving from Chicago in the next couple of days. He stayed behind to button everything up before heading home," Koi explained. "Jennie, you'll never know how much we appreciate his help. He stood by Osi the whole time, and he was instrumental in securing that skillful attorney to represent him."

"Despite his drinking habit, he can be quite brilliant at times."

Koi nodded. "Osi would still be sitting in that jail if it wasn't for him. I'm so glad all this is behind us. Come on, let me see the baby."

Koi and Jennie walked to the nursery where little Jacob lay snug in his crib. Jennie pulled back the covers to show a healthy baby boy. His little round head was covered with straight black hair and his skin was light brown.

"Oh, Jennie, he's beautiful! I can hardly wait until he's big enough to play with Kash."

Jennie frowned. "Why didn't you bring Kash with you?"

"Gentle Woman wanted me to leave him at Marietta Place with her and Rose. It's a bit nippy outside, and Gentle Woman is so protective lately. Where's Matthew?"

"He's at the law office. He's been holding down the fort while Michael's been gone. He never studied to become an attorney, but he sure knows a lot about the law. I guess some of his father's knowledge rubbed off on him."

"Ples said Amos Brooks was arrested for killing Francis Kirby. Have you heard anything about it?"

Jennie pulled the covers back up over the baby. "Yes. Matthew mentioned it last night when he got home. I'm sure he'll discuss it with Michael when he gets back from Chicago. They'll probably be representing Amos *pro bono*. That family is as poor as church mice. I feel bad for them. I don't believe for one minute that Amos could kill anyone."

Koi shook her head in agreement. "I wonder how Sally and the kids are faring. We should take up a collection of food and get it to them."

"I was thinking the same thing. Maybe the church group can do something to help. I'll announce their dilemma on Sunday morning and see what can be done." Jennie said.

Koi removed several silver dollars from her delicately beaded reticule. "Here, take these." She handed the money to Jennie. Quickly changing the subject, she asked, "How does Mrs. McIver like her little brown grandson?"

"Oh … she is proud as punch. You'd never know that she was prejudiced against Indians not so long ago. She thinks he's the sweetest thing in the world. She drops by every day to see how he's doing. Mrs. McIver would practically live here if I let her. Matthew and I've been longing for Michael to get home so she can focus on him and not be so preoccupied with the baby." Jennie smiled. "I'll heat some water for tea, and we can chat about what went on in Chicago."

Koi went into the parlor, took a seat, and waited. Jennie soon came into the room, carrying a tray of aromatic teas, a teapot with hot water, and two fancy China teacups. She set the tray on the tea table then turned to Koi. "You don't have black clothes on. Shouldn't you be in mourning?"

Koi didn't answer right away. She casually reached for a teacup, dropped in a few tea leaves, then added hot water from the pot. "Jennie, I didn't wear black at the trial nor anytime I was in Chicago. I refuse to mourn Neville Cooper. He was my husband in name only, and I prefer to put this all behind me and not be reminded of that period in my life. As far as I'm concerned, his long-time girlfriend, Claire Dubois, was more of a wife to him than me."

"Claire Dubois? Who's she?"

"It's a long story." Koi stared into her teacup. She swirled the mixture around in a circle with her spoon and watched the leaves change position. "I've heard that some people can read tea leaves," she said softly, trying to change the subject. "I wish I knew how to decipher them. If I could, maybe I could foresee our future."

"We're not supposed to know our future. Only heathens believe in such things."

Koi rolled her eyes.

"What about Claire Dubois?" Jennie persisted.

Koi sighed. "Please swear on a stack of Bibles you won't tell anyone what I'm about to tell you. Eventually, everything will come out in the open, but for now, please keep my secret."

Jennie made an **X** on her chest with her finger. "Cross my heart and hope to die." It was something she and Koi always did when they told each other secrets.

"Okay, then," Koi continued. "Neville had a girlfriend named Claire, who lived in Chicago. One afternoon Claire and I met in the hotel foyer and had tea together in the tearoom. We talked about Neville. She said she had been his companion for years. She thought that someday they'd be married. He told her

11

he would marry her when he returned after completing his job with the Dawes Commission. Claire found out about our marriage and that Neville had a son when she read an article in the newspaper after his death. It came as a total shock to her. She told me that she was curious to meet me, so she came to the hotel."

"I bet you were devastated to find out Neville had a girlfriend."

"Not really. I never loved Neville, so I couldn't have cared less. Obviously, Claire wanted to see Kash. She was probably relieved when she saw that my baby had the appearance of a full-blood Indian with no resemblance whatsoever to Neville." A smile crossed Koi's lips. "We talked a bit in the foyer and then she invited me into the tearoom. Over tea I explained that Neville and I had never consummated our marriage, that I married him to fulfill a promise to my dying mother, and that Kash was not Neville's son."

Jennie gasped upon hearing that unexpected piece of news.

Ignoring Jennie's reaction, Koi continued. "I went on to tell Claire that I was sure Neville loved her and only married me to secure his trust among the Indians. We left the tearoom cordially, with an understanding that we had both been pawns in Neville's game." Koi took a deep breath, sat back in her chair, and began to sip her tea. There was a long pause before she spoke again.

"At the trial Claire swore that Neville shot himself and she said she saw him do it. Osi might have received a hanging sentence if she hadn't testified on his behalf. Claire saved his life." Suddenly, Koi changed her demeanor. "Actually, I like Claire and think we could be good friends. I've invited her to come to Okla Chuka for a visit."

"Koi, let me get this straight. Kash is not Neville's child? Neville had a girlfriend in Chicago, you met her, and now you've invited her to visit you?"

"Yes. I think you'll like her too, once you get to know her."

Jennie took a sip of tea and stared off into space, trying to soak it all in. Hearing a faint whimper, she stood and turned to walk toward the nursery. "I better check on Jacob."

12

Chapter Two

Ardmore

When Koi returned to Marietta Place, she found John and Osi sitting in the parlor, smoking and discussing how they could get Amos released from jail. She gave them a quick wave when she passed through.

"Kash is with Gentle Woman in the parlor," John said, returning Koi's greeting.

Osi snuffed out his cigar. "I need to get to the ranch in a day or so. I hope nothing drastic has happened since I've been gone."

"Ples does a good job overseeing everything at Okla Chuka," John said, "but it'll be good to get back home. And there's not much we can do for Amos until Michael gets back from Chicago. Hopefully, we'll get information about Kirby when we talk to our friends."

"Matthew might know something." Changing the subject, Osi continued, "I'm eager to find out how Luther is handling his job as governor."

"It's such a shame the Progressives are taking over. It won't be long now before our land will be divided up. I bet it galls Matthew to know his brother-in-law is the head of that faction," John said.

Osi stood to leave. "I think I'll make a trip over to the law office. I'll see y'all in a couple hours."

◊◊◊

A large printed sign hung over the door to the McIver Law Office. When Osi stepped inside, Matthew rose to his feet from behind a large mahogany desk. "I'm so glad you're back," Matthew said.

"It's good to be home. I want to congratulate you on your baby boy," Osi replied enthusiastically. "We heard the news from your father. And speaking of your father, I sure appreciate all he did for me while I was in jail."

Matthew pulled a straight back chair next to his desk. "Have a seat. My father drinks a lot of whiskey, but he's a smart man."

"Without his help, I'd still be sitting in that Chicago jail … or worse, hung by now. I don't know how I can ever repay him."

"He doesn't expect you to repay him." Matthew opened a light-colored birchwood humidor and offered Osi a cigar. "I guess you've heard about Amos Brooks being arrested."

"Yes, Ples told us last night. I wonder what really happened."

"I don't think anyone knows. When my father gets back, we'll discuss how to help Amos."

"He's in good hands with you and Michael. Let me know if there's anything I can do." Osi's eyes scanned the room. "This place sure looks different!" Papers were neatly stacked on the desk and rows of modern law books were alphabetized along the bookshelves. "I must say, Matthew, you've made a big improvement by getting this place organized."

"It wasn't easy. Father saved every scrap of paper he ever wrote on. The hard part was deciding what to throw away and what to keep. He'll probably have a hissy fit when he gets back, but at least now we can find what we need and not spend hours looking through piles of papers stacked everywhere." Matthew chuckled then frowned. "Osi, have you heard anything about representatives from the Five Civilized Tribes getting together to talk about statehood?"

"Matter of fact, I have. I sat next to a Cherokee man on the train up near Guthrie. His name is Isaac Roberts and he was on his way to Tahlequah to attend a meeting."

Matthew fumbled through a stack of papers on his desk. "I read something in the *Daily Ardmoreite* about several tribal representatives holding a meeting awhile back. The article said they don't want to be part of the new state called Oklahoma. They want Indian Territory to become a separate state. I can't seem to find the piece now, but the way it was written, it seems like the editor is in favor of combining both territories."

Osi stood and walked to the window. Looking out, he said, "You and I both know if that happens, the Indians of the Five Nations will be outnumbered on every issue. I think we should have a say-so in this matter. Do you have any idea who's representing the Chickasaws?"

"The article didn't say, but I don't think the Chickasaws had anyone at the meeting. Luther never mentioned anything to me," Matthew said. "As a matter of fact, Jennie and I hardly ever see her brother. Getting elected Governor of the Chickasaw Nation has gone to his head."

"I better send a telegram to Isaac Roberts in Tahlequah. I'd like to attend their next meeting," Osi said with determination. He bid Matthew goodbye, promising to talk to him again soon.

On the way back to Marietta Place, Osi said a prayer to Ababinnili and asked for guidance in this matter. He gave thanks to the Creator for all his blessings and asked that he might have the wisdom and strength to continue to fight for Chickasaw sovereignty and his people.

Jennie's House

Mrs. McIver, Jennie's mother-in-law, knocked on the front door. She was there for her daily visit to see baby Jacob. Her red hair was now streaked with gray, and she still pulled it back into a tight chignon at the back of her head. And she continued to dust herself with the same lilac-perfumed powder that was unmistakably her.

"Come on in, Mother," Jennie said as she opened the door. "Would you mind staying with Jacob while I take this basket of food to Amos Brooks' wife?"

"You know I always want an excuse to spend more time with that little one," Mrs. McIver eagerly replied.

"Koi was here earlier and we talked about needing to

check on Sally and the kids since Amos is still locked up in jail. I plan on seeing what the church can do for them on Sunday, but for now this basket of food should do. I'm sure Koi and Gentle Woman will pitch in a few things too."

Jennie packed her basket in her small buggy and hurried toward Marietta Place. Once there she slowed the buggy to a halt and tied the reins to the hitching post. She ran up the porch steps and was greeted at the door by Koi.

"I got to thinking after you left that maybe we should take Sally and the Brooks children some food today," Jennie told Koi. "Do you want to go with me to deliver it?"

"Sure, come on in. I'll see if Gentle Woman has anything she can add to your supplies."

Jennie stepped inside the house and saw Rose carrying Kash down the hall. "Wait, Rose, let me see Kash." Rose handed the baby to Jennie.

"Oh, my goodness gracious! He has really grown while y'all been gone."

"Yes, he has, Miz Jackson. Oh … I mean Miz McIver," Rose corrected herself.

Jennie smiled and cooed at Kash for the few minutes it took for Koi and Gentle Woman to come from the kitchen with arms full of food and set it all on a side table near the front door.

"I'll see if Ples has a box we can use. I'll be right back," Koi said.

"Nice seeing you again, Mrs. Nance," Jennie greeted Gentle Woman. "Where's Mr. Prichett?"

"He's taking a nap. That trip to Chicago sure took a toll on him. He hasn't caught up with his rest yet." Gentle Woman glanced at the food on the table. "I'm glad you two girls are taking food to the Brooks family. They need all the help they can get. Be careful on that road though. It's got so many ruts and gullies, it's easy to break an axle."

"We'll be extra careful," Koi said, overhearing Gentle Woman's warning as she returned from the stable.

The women quickly loaded the food into the wooden box Koi got from Ples. She grabbed her coat from the hall and the girls scampered out the door with the food.

Brooks House

Jennie turned the buggy onto the path that led up to the Brooks' ramshackle farmhouse. A dozen or more guinea hens announced their arrival with a racket that would raise the dead.

Hearing the commotion, Sally came out the front door, wiping her hands on her dirty, threadbare apron. She ran her hands through her matted hair, trying to spiffy herself up for the two ladies who had come to call.

"How are you doing, Sally?" Koi asked, stepping down from the buggy.

"I reckon we're okay. Do you know when Amos is comin' home?"

"Osi went to see him today, and the McIvers are on the case. They'll have him home soon," Koi prophesied. "Where are the children?"

Sally hollered for her kids to come see Miz Koi and Miz Jennie, and ten or so little ragamuffins came running from all directions. It was as though they appeared out of nowhere.

"Children, we're doing everything we can for your father. Hopefully, he'll be home soon," Koi said.

Jennie climbed down from the buggy and started unloading the food. "Sally, this should be enough to last you for a few days. I'll be seeing the ladies at church on Sunday, and I'm sure they'll be delivering some staples to you next week."

"Y'all are good people. I knowed Amos would be proud of all y'all give us."

The women knew Sally didn't have words to express her feelings. This was the only way she knew how to thank them.

On the way back to Marietta Place, Jennie kept thinking about all the things Koi had told her. Finally, she slowed the horse to a walk and asked, "Koi, have you thought about what people will say when they find out that Kash isn't Neville's son?"

"Well, I was hoping to keep it a secret until Kash got older. Time has a way of smoothing things."

It was just like her not to think about it, Jennie thought. Koi would brush it off like always and concern herself with it another day.

Marietta Place

Jennie bade Koi goodbye and continued down the road. When the buggy had disappeared from sight, Koi stepped inside the house and found Osi and her father talking in the parlor. "Hi, I'm home," she announced.

"Koi, come in here," John said. "We've decided to leave for Tishomingo at the crack of dawn. I'd like to have the buggy loaded by evening. It'll be good to get back to the ranch and take care of business."

Osi nodded in agreement.

"Goodness, I'd better get at it," Koi said. "I'll find Rose and get her to help." She found her in the guest room, sitting in the cane back rocking chair, trying to get Kash to sleep. "Rose, it's time for us to start packing. We'll be leaving first thing in the morning."

Koi picked up Kash's soiled clothing and plunked them in a basket. *I've not had one moment alone with Osi since we've arrived.* She frowned at the thought.

◊◊◊

At sundown John suggested they should all go to bed. Tomorrow would be a very busy day for everyone. Koi went to the guest room she was sharing with Kash and Rose. John and Ples were bunking in an unfinished side room, and Osi said he preferred to sleep on the parlor floor.

"Here, Osi." Gentle Woman handed him a blanket and pillow before retiring to her room. "I sure am going to miss y'all when you leave."

"Mother, you should come with us."

"This is my home now, Osi. Besides, I like the luxury of running water," she grinned.

◊◊◊

Koi lay wide awake, staring at the ceiling for hours after everyone had gone to sleep. Rose's heavy breathing kept her awake as she lay next to her in the same bed. She was thankful Kash was settled and sleeping in his crib.

She longed for Osi to hold her and make love to her. These pleasant thoughts filled her mind until they became a tangled blur and she drifted off to sleep.

Standing on her porch the next morning, Gentle Woman waved goodbye to her family as they drove away from Marietta Place. Koi blew her a final kiss as the buggy pulled away from the gate.

The family took the road east to Tishomingo by way of Greasy Bend. They could have taken the route north through Sorghum Flats and Price Falls and across the Arbuckle Mountains, but they were not looking for a scenic view this time.

The sun was setting when the buggy pulled into the stables at the Greasy Bend Inn.

"I'll be glad when spring gets here. I've been freezing since we left Ardmore," Koi said as she removed the lap robe and stepped down from the buggy. Osi tried to get to her side before she exited, but he wasn't fast enough. She was already scurrying toward the front door.

"I guess she's in an all-fired hurry to get warm," Osi said, lifting Kash from Rose's lap. Osi held the baby with one arm and helped Rose down with the other. He cradled Kash, hesitating before giving him back to Rose. This was the first time he had held *his* son. Memories flashed back to the night Kash was born. He had silently slipped into Koi's room while she was sleeping and gently pulled back the blanket covering the baby. To him all babies looked the same, but Koi's baby was special. Osi had vowed he would forever love Koi's son like his own.

When Koi revealed that *he* was Kash's father, he'd heard the words, but the realization that the boy was *his blood* had not hit him. Now, however, holding his son, Osi was overcome with emotion. To conceal the tears that had welled up in his eyes, he quickly handed Kash to Rose. "Get him warm inside while we bring in the luggage."

19

Koi hurried to the desk clerk before the others. "We would all like separate rooms."

"How many, ma'am?"

"Five."

He pointed to the hotel logbook. "Sign here. We don't get many travelers this time of year. I believe we can accommodate y'all.

Koi was writing her name when Rose came in the door with Kash. "Rose, please take Kash by the fire and get him warm. I'm going upstairs to check out our rooms." Koi turned to the attendant and instructed, "My father will be in shortly to pay. He's taking the horses and buggy to the stable."

The clerk nodded, handing Koi the room keys.

◊◊◊

Koi went from room to room to see if any two were connected. "Yes!" she said aloud when she found what she was looking for. Separating the keys and checking to see which key matched which room, she put Osi's and her room keys in her left hand to make sure Osi received the one that adjoined her room.

She returned downstairs just as her father, Osi, and Ples walked inside. "I've already signed us in. Here's the keys." Koi gave Osi his first then one to her father, followed by those for Rose and Ples.

"Rose, I want Kash to sleep in your room tonight. I'm exhausted and need a good night's sleep."

"Of course, Miz Koi."

"I'll see if they have a crib they can bring to your room."

"Yes, ma'am."

"Is anyone else as hungry as I am?" Koi asked. Everyone nodded. "Rose, I'll have dinner brought to your room. And I'll see what they have that Kash can eat. I hope they have mashed potatoes and peas. They're his favorites."

"Thank you, Miz Koi. I believe I'll go take Kash to the room now and change his soakers."

20

Koi leaned over and gave her son a kiss on the forehead. "Good night, *Iskunosi,* little one. See you in the morning."

John wasn't sure if the clerk would allow a black man in the dining room. To save Ples the possible embarrassment, he said, "Ples, I'll have your supper sent to your room."

Koi, Osi, and John strolled into the dining room after washing up. They were impressed with the meal of fried chicken, mashed potatoes and gravy provided at this little wide spot in the road. After dinner and saying goodnight, the travelers went to their respective rooms.

Koi waited until everyone was asleep before she opened the door between her room and Osi's.

◊◊◊

Osi pretended to be asleep as Koi inched her way to his bed. He heard her feeling for the covers in the dark and felt her slide under. She scooted over and pressed her warm naked body next to his. He had been waiting for her.

It was after midnight before Koi went back to her own room.

21

Chapter Three

Gentle Woman stood on the porch at Marietta Place long after the Pritchett's buggy drove out the gate and down the road. She was getting used to the family being together and felt a twinge of sadness at seeing them leave.

It was not like her to feel sorry for herself, so she decided to get busy. Spotting the stack of split wood by the front door, she picked up a log, carried it into the house, loaded it into the wood stove, and used the poker to stoke the fire before warming her hands near the flames. Then she walked into the kitchen, lifted her apron from its wall hook, and put it on over her winter coat.

Gentle Woman loved her chickens, so gathering the eggs and tending them would be the first chore of the day. She went to the stable and scooped several cups of feed into her apron. Back outside, she threw handfuls of corn on the ground and enjoyed watching the fowl scratch and peck as they found each tiny morsel. Shaking her apron to make sure there was nothing left, she gathered the empty cloth into a bundle and collected the eggs from the nests.

When she turned to walk back to the kitchen, she saw smoke pouring out the back door as fire engulfed the house. Flames shot from the windows and began lapping at the roof. She loosened her hold on the apron, letting the eggs drop to the ground, and ran toward the house as fast as her aged body would allow. *I have to save the cedar box!*

Gentle Woman rushed up the steps to the front door. She quickly flung it open, stepping aside to let the smoke and flames billow out. Dropping down on her hands and knees, she crawled into the house and inched her way down the hall toward her bedroom. The fire had not reached that far, but the entire house was filled with black sooty smoke. The thick, acrid fumes caused her to cough violently. Pulling her apron to her face as a makeshift mask, she snaked her way to the far end of the house. Disoriented and confused, she could hardly breathe. Her lungs were ready to explode. She moved frantically, trying to find the door to her bedroom.

Finding it at last and crawling inside, she saw a dim, foggy light in the distance. She inched her way toward the faint glow to discover it was the window. She stood erect and reached her arm above her head to feel for the shelf. She knew the box had to be there. Running her fingers across the edge, she touched the corner of the chest.

Gentle Woman grabbed the chest and held it next to her bosom while struggling to get the window open. It wouldn't budge. The wall beside her was hot. The fire was coming close. Adjusting the box in one hand, she used the elbow of her free arm to break the glass. She managed to climb out and crawl several feet away before collapsing in the yard.

The thick black cloud of smoke rising above Marietta Place had been seen by the nearest neighbors, and it wasn't long before the community bell rang loud and clear. The volunteer firemen were quickly on the scene.

"Mrs. Nance! Mrs. Nance!" a fireman called, trying to get her to come awake. He took the box from her clenched arms and set it on the ground beside her.

"Where's my cedar box?" Gentle Woman coughed then moaned before falling back into unconsciousness.

By now several people had come to help. Mrs. McIver, in her nightgown and robe with her hair in paper rollers, shouted to the fireman, "Take her to my house!" She made her way across the yard to where Gentle Woman lay. "Is she burned?"

"I don't think so," the fireman kneeling beside Gentle Woman mumbled. "She's got a nasty cut on her leg though. We have to stop the bleeding." He tightly pressed her skirt along the gash on her thigh. "She's lucky she didn't get more cuts. Her heavy coat was good protection."

The fireman instructed a person nearby to fetch the doctor and meet them at the McIver place. He picked up Gentle

Woman and carried her to the back of Mrs. McIver's two-seater buggy then hopped in beside her to hold her steady. "By the time we get to your house, Mrs. McIver, the doctor should be waiting," he said.

"Wait! Where's her cedar box?" Mrs. McIver asked, knowing how important the box was to Gentle Woman. She jumped from the buggy, retrieved it from the ground where Gentle Woman had been lying, then climbed back into the driver's seat. She took the whip from its holder and flung the braided leather strap above the horse's head, making it snap loudly. The horse bolted, running for home.

The doctor was waiting on the front steps when they arrived. Mrs. McIver rushed into the house to show the fireman where to take Gentle Woman. "Bring her this way and put her in the guest room."

The man carried Gentle Woman to the bed, leaving a trail of blood. By now she was breathing easier but was still not awake. However, the bumpy ride had helped to clear some of the smoke from her lungs, and she began to stir, appearing to be coming out of it, when the doctor began examining her.

"My cedar box ... my cedar box ..." Gentle Woman kept saying in a faint voice.

"Don't worry. I have it right here," Mrs. McIver assured her. She placed it on the bed then took Gentle Woman's hand and touched it to the box so she could feel that it was safe and sound.

Gentle Woman opened her eyes ever so slightly. "Violet," she whispered before passing out again.

The doctor stitched her leg and finished his examination. "I think she'll be all right. We've got the bleeding stopped. But I'm concerned that she's breathed too much smoke. It may develop into pneumonia. Keep her warm, make sure she continues to cough, and try to get as much out of her lungs as she can when she wakes up," he instructed Violet, closing his black bag. "Have someone come get me if she doesn't rally soon or if her leg starts bleeding again. And be sure to keep that wound clean."

"Thank you both," Mrs. McIver said, nodding to the physician and the fireman before quickly returning to her patient.

24

By now word had spread that Marietta Place had burned down. Matthew and Jennie, with baby Jacob, rushed to Matthew's parents' house when they heard. Mrs. McIver had already spongebathed and dressed Gentle Woman in a clean nightgown before they arrived.

"What happened?" Matthew asked his mother.

"I don't think anyone knows for sure. The firemen think a spark from the stove started it. When the fire reached the kerosene lamp, it exploded. I'm sure they'll be asking Gentle Woman what she thinks happened when she gets her senses about her. She rallied a little when I was bathing her, but she's so weak it may be some time before we know anything."

"We have to let Osi know. Maybe I can catch them at the Greasy Bend Inn," Matthew said. "I'll go to the telegraph office and send a message."

◇◇◇

"The Greasy Bend Inn doesn't have telegraph service," the Western Operator explained. "But you could send a telegram to Tishomingo and then hire a courier to ride back towards Ardmore and intercept the buggy somewhere along the road."

"Yes. That sounds like a plan. Let's do it," Matthew agreed. He then dictated his message to the operator.

◇◇◇

It was just before dawn when a loud knock was heard throughout the Inn. Someone was banging on Osi's door.

"Mr. Nance! Mr. Nance!" the hotel clerk yelled. "You have a message."

Osi jumped out of bed and quickly slipped into his trousers before opening the door. "Yes?"

The clerk handed Osi an ochre-colored envelope. "Here's a telegram for you. The messenger said it was urgent."

25

The only light in the hall was a dim flicker coming from the kerosene lamp the clerk held. "Please turn up the wick so I can read it," Osi requested as he ripped open the envelope.

```
TO JORDAN OSI NANCE
TISHOMINGO COUNTY
TISHOMINGO INDIAN TERRITORY

FIRE AT MARIETTA PLACE STOP
GENTLE WOMAN ALIVE STOP
SHE IS AT MY PARENTS HOUSE STOP
COME IMMEDIATELY STOP

FROM MATTHEW MCIVER
PICKENS COUNTY
ARDMORE INDIAN TERRITORY
```

Osi read the telegram and stuffed it into his trousers. "Tell the stable boy to get the buggy ready," he instructed. "I'll need to rent a horse and saddle too. I have to get to Ardmore as quickly as possible, so give me the fastest horse you have." He stepped back into his room and lit the lamp so he could see to gather his belongings.

Awakened by the commotion, Koi and John hurried into Osi's room. "What was that knocking all about?" John asked.

"We have to get back to Ardmore immediately! Marietta Place burned down," Osi said. "Mother is alive, but Matthew didn't say if she was burned or not. He said she was at his parents' house."

"Oh, no!" Koi cried. She ran to Osi and threw her arms around his neck.

He reached up and unlocked her grip. "Koi, we have to move fast. Get your things together. Tell Rose and Ples to do the same. The stable boy is getting the buggy ready now. I'm going to ride on ahead so I can make better time. I'll see y'all at the McIver place." He gave Koi a quick peck on the cheek, picked up his satchel, flung it over his back, and hurried down the hall and out the door.

The sun was starting to peek over the eastern horizon, announcing the beginning of a new day, when Osi turned the horse away from the stable and onto the road leading to Ardmore. He gave the stallion a swift kick in the flanks and plenty of loose reins. It took off running.

◊◊◊

The horse was frothing at the mouth when Osi arrived at the McIvers' house. He knew just how hard he could ride an animal before it collapsed, and he had pushed this one almost to the limit. Although he was anxious to see his mother, he immediately took the horse to the stable for a small amount of water and a quick rub down.

By the time Osi finished taking care of the horse, the sun had set. He could see light from the kerosene lamps streaming through the windows as he hurried to the house and knocked on the door. "Mrs. McIver!" he yelled.

Violet came to the door and welcomed him inside. "Come on in, Osi. I'm so glad you're here. Gentle Woman had quite an ordeal, but she's doing better. The doctor says she needs to cough to keep from getting pneumonia." Violet kept talking as she escorted Osi down the hall. "She was able to break a window and get out before the flames reached her, so she didn't get burned. But she breathed in a lot of smoke and she has a pretty bad cut on her leg from the broken glass. A fireman found her in the yard, clutching her cedar box."

Violet opened the bedroom door ever so slightly and peeked in to see if Gentle Woman was awake. "She's still asleep," she whispered, closing the door. "She drank some chicken broth for supper. It would probably be best if we let her sleep while you get settled. Come, I'll show you to the room where you can stay."

Osi followed her down the hall to the far end of the house where Mrs. McIver opened the door to a bedroom. "Make yourself comfortable then come to the kitchen when you're ready," she said. "I'll heat the chicken and dumplins'."

27

Osi was exhausted and glad to have some time to clean up and relax. He was relieved to know that his mother was alive and well and that all she needed was rest and time to recuperate. He sat down on the feather bed to pray. He gave thanks to the Great Creator in heaven for sparing his mother's life. He closed his eyes and continued to pray for Koi and Kash and all his many blessings. While praying, he drifted off to sleep.

Chapter Four

The sound of men's voices woke Osi from his nap. He opened the bedroom door and walked toward the noise to find Matthew and Michael sitting at the kitchen table. "When did you get here?" Osi asked.

"The train arrived about an hour ago and Matthew picked me up," Michael said, stuffing another bite of dumplings in his mouth. "It sure is good to be home. Matthew's been catching me up on all the news. I'm sorry to hear about your mother's house burning down. It's a blessing she got out safely."

"Yes. We can be thankful for that."

"Osi, your mother wants to see you now," Violet said as she walked into the kitchen. She seems to be getting better by the minute."

"Excuse me, gentlemen, I'll be back soon." Osi looked at their plates of food and began to salivate. "That chicken and dumplings sure looks good."

When Osi quietly opened the door to his mother's room, he found her sitting up in bed, propped with several pillows. Seeing Osi, she smiled. "Come on in."

Osi was thrilled to see her wide awake and talking. He went to her bedside, leaned over, and kissed her on the forehead. "I'm so glad you're alright. What happened?"

"Well, after y'all left, I threw a log on the fire and went out to gather eggs. I was headed back to the kitchen when I saw the house in flames. A spark must have popped through the screen and caught the rug. All I could think of at the moment was saving my cedar box."

"Mother, I know it means the world to you, but it wasn't worth risking your life." Osi grimaced at the thought of losing his

29

mother.

"You don't understand. I have to keep it safe," Gentle Woman said without further explanation.

He knew there was no use arguing with her. All that mattered was she was now safe and a tragedy had been avoided.

"Violet said you haven't eaten yet. She made a good supper. You better go get your fill." Gentle Woman paused. "I think I'll go to sleep now. I'll see you in the morning."

Osi said goodnight, twisted the lamp wick down, and walked from the room. By the time he returned to the kitchen, Mrs. McIver was generously spooning hot food onto his plate.

"That smells mighty good, Violet. I'm famished." Osi took the plate and joined the men at the table. "Do either one of you have any idea how we can get Amos out of jail?"

"We were just discussing that," Michael said.

"It doesn't look good. He had good reason to kill Francis Kirby," Matthew added.

"He might have had good reason to kill him, but we all know he didn't do it," Osi said.

Michael nodded. "I consulted with James Whitley after y'all left Chicago. We talked about the papers Amos found incriminating Neville Cooper and Francis Kirby as being part of the Syndicate. He said the Feds wouldn't be sending investigators if they didn't think this was of the upmost importance. I think Neville and Francis were just two of many nefarious characters stealing Indian lands."

"We can talk about it tomorrow." Matthew stood and walked to the door. "It's getting late and I need to get home. Good night, y'all."

◊◊◊

It was after midnight when the Prichett's buggy approached Ardmore.

"Ples, we'll be staying at the hotel," John said. "McIver's house isn't big enough to accommodate all of us. Let's stop at the front before pulling around to the stable."

"Yes, sir." Ples tugged back on the reins. "Whoa, boy," he called.

John stepped from the buggy and helped the women down. "Y'all go inside, I'll be there in a minute."

Koi entered the hotel, followed by Rose carrying Kash. "There's a bench over there." Koi pointed to a seat. She stepped to the desk and rang the bell. When no one appeared immediately, she walked back to the bench where Rose was waiting. "Here, let me hold Kash," she offered. "You've been burdened with him almost the entire way."

"That's alright, Miz Koi. I think he's used to sleeping in my lap."

Koi smiled and lifted a sleeping Kash from her, noticing for the first time that her long-time servant was getting on in age. Tonight she appeared haggard and her arms looked limp. Koi saw her open and close her hands a few times to get the circulation going after handing over the baby.

Rose had been with the Prichetts long before Koi was born and had taken care of Koi herself as a baby. There was no one Koi trusted more with the care of her son than Rose.

"Well, that's taken care of," John said, interrupting her thoughts as he walked into the hotel, carrying their overnight satchels. "Ples will bunk in the stable. First thing in the morning, he'll hitch a ride to Marietta Place to see if Gentle Woman's horse and the buggy survived the ordeal. I'm hoping the firemen were able to keep the barn from burning down."

"Oh … I hope Bess is okay." Koi bit her lip. "I love that horse."

"If they *are* safe, Ples will bring them here or to McIver's stable until Osi decides what to do with them." John stepped to the desk and paid for two rooms.

When he signed his name in the logbook, the clerk asked, "Are you Mr. John Prichett?"

"Yes," he replied.

"Here's a message for you."

"Thank you," John tore open the envelope and read the short note. *Gentle Woman is good. You don't need to come until morning. Matthew McIver.* He smiled and put the paper in his pocket. "Please have a baby bed put in her room," John

31

requested and pointed toward Koi. He assumed Rose would be sleeping with Koi. They often slept together in the same bed.

Turning to the women, John handed Koi her room key and then asked the attendant, "Which way?"

The clerk pointed down the hall and John was relieved he didn't have to carry their satchels upstairs. "That note was from Matthew," John told Koi as they walked toward their rooms. "He said Gentle Woman is doing good, so we don't need to rush." John sat the luggage in Koi's room and gave her a good night peck on the cheek. "I'll have the buggy ready for us to go after breakfast."

◊◊◊

The next morning a blinding fog covered the entire town. The Prichetts were forced to wait for it to lift before they could travel, so it was early afternoon before they arrived at the McIvers'.

"I'm glad to see Bess is all right," John said when he spotted Ples in the barn, grooming her. "Y'all go on in the house. I'll be there after I get the horses unhitched."

When Koi knocked on the door, with Rose standing behind her holding Kash, Mrs. McIver greeted them with a big smile. "Bless your little hearts. Come on in. You must feel like you've been whipped after being on the road so long."

Koi held the door for Rose and Kash then stepped inside behind them. When she saw Gentle Woman sitting in the parlor, she ran to her and threw her arms around her. "I'm so glad to see you're not burned. I was worried to death about you."

"I'm fine. Violet's taking good care of me."

"I hope you women will excuse me, but I need to tend to my cooking in the kitchen. I'll leave you alone so you can get caught up with your talking," Mrs. McIver said.

"Come over here and take a seat next to me." Gentle Woman pointed to an empty chair.

Rose was left standing in the middle of the room, fidgeting with a squirming baby. "Excuse me, Miz Koi. Do you think I could take Kash for a ride in his perambulator? He's mighty antsy today."

"I think that's a great idea. I'll tell Father to unload it from the buggy."

Gentle Woman smiled as Koi left to find her father. "Bring Kash over here, please," she requested. When Rose got close, Gentle Woman reached out and grabbed the baby's little hand. "He's such a fine boy," she said with love.

Koi entered the room, letting the door slam shut. "You can take Kash for his ride now. Father has the baby buggy unloaded and ready to go," she told Rose then sat down next to Gentle Woman. "Now, where were we?" she asked.

Gentle Woman sat silently until Rose and Kash left the room then she leaned close to Koi and whispered. "Have you thought about what you'll do when you get back to Tishomingo?"

"Someday I'd like to start a school of art and music for Chickasaw children. I haven't mentioned this to Osi or Father, but it's something I'd like to do."

"I think that's a fine idea. I know Osi will think it's admirable of you to want to educate our children."

"I also want us to have a church wedding, but isn't it too soon after Neville's death? Aren't we supposed to wait a year?" Koi asked.

"That *is* customary," Gentle Woman nodded.

Koi crossed her legs and sat up straight. "I haven't told Father that Kash is Osi's son." There was a moment of awkward silence. "You've known all along haven't you, Mother?"

"Yes, and your father knows."

"Are you sure?"

"Yes. I told him. We had a long conversation about it in Chicago. He knows you love each other. It's obvious! I told him I performed a Chickasaw wedding ceremony, uniting you both before you married Neville. I even showed him the contents of the cedar box."

Koi gasped. "What did he say?"

"Nothing. I explained I had dried Osi's and your placentas at birth and saved them by wrapping each separately in heavy gauze before placing them in the cedar box. When I opened it years later, the afterbirths were twisted into a knot impossible to untangle. John wanted to see for himself, so I showed him. Koi, your father knows our Chickasaw beliefs. He knows this is a sign."

Gentle Woman took a deep breath and continued. "It means that nothing on this earth can separate you. You and Osi were promised to each other long before your spirits entered your earthly bodies." She sat back in the chair and closed her eyes.

"Oh, Mother," Koi sighed. She was too emotional to continue the conversation any further.

John walked into the house by way of the back door and found Mrs. McIver preparing vegetables for lunch. "Hello, Violet. I want to thank you for taking care of Gentle Woman."

"It's my pleasure, John. We all have to take care of each other from time to time. Remember when she took us in and cooked for us when we had that awful tornado?"

"Don't think any of us could forget about that storm." John looked around. "Where's Osi?"

"He went with Michael down to the law office to meet Matthew. They were going to try to get Amos out of jail."

"When did Michael get back from Chicago?"

"Last night," Violet said. "He sent a telegram to Matthew saying when to pick him up. I don't know what time Osi and Michael went to bed. They were still talking and smoking when I retired. And this morning they were gone before I got up."

"How's Gentle Woman?" John asked.

"Getting' better all the time. She and Koi are in the parlor."

He found the women chatting. "Hello, ladies."

"Father, look at Gentle Woman. She's fine."

"That's good.' John patted Gentle Woman on the hand. "I was concerned that you might be laid up for a while."

"Another day or so and I should be back to my old self."

"Ples went to Marietta Place this morning. He said there's nothing left of the house, but we can be glad the stable didn't burn. Praise the Lord you've got Bess and the buggy."

"Yes, thank you, Creator." Gentle Woman bowed her head.

John stood, rubbing his chin nervously. "I have a proposition for you."

"What are you up to now, John Pritchett?" Gentle Woman asked.

"We've gotten pretty used to being together all the time, and Kash needs his granny living close by, so I'm asking you to come and live at Okla Chuka with us. I won't take no for an answer."

Gentle Woman looked thoughtful. "I don't know what I'm going to do. I didn't get a chance to talk to Osi before he left this morning, so I have no idea what he wants to do with the property here in Ardmore. I appreciate the offer and I will consider it, but I have to talk to him first."

Koi had been sitting quietly, listening to their conversation, but now she couldn't resist speaking up. "Mother, please come live with us," she begged.

"We'll see."

"I'm going to leave you lovely women now and go down to the law office and see if I can get in the way," John said jokingly. "See y'all later."

Osi and Michael drove by Marietta Place before going to the law office. "Looks like nothin's left but the stable and chicken yard," Osi observed. "Do you or Matthew want the chickens?"

"If he doesn't want 'em, I'll take 'em."

"There's lots of food in the cellar and smokehouse. I'm gonna see if Mother wants to give it to the Brooks family. I'm sure they could use it." Osi continued, "When we get to your building, I'm going to walk to the abstract office and let them know the lot is now for sale. I'm taking Mother back home to the ranch."

John drove his buggy to the McIver law office where he found the men sitting around the desk, puffing the Cuban cigars Michael had brought from Chicago.

"Hey, John, come in and join us." Michael thrust an open humidor at him.

"Thank you, I don't mind if I do." John took a cigar from the box, lifted it to his nose, and took a deep breath to smell the aroma of the sweet tobacco. "There's nothing like a fine Cuban cigar to start the day."

Matthew pulled another chair near the desk.

"What have y'all decided to do about Amos?" John asked.

"I think the first thing we need to do is post bail. Then we can concentrate on how we're going to prove his innocence," Michael answered.

Chapter Five

"It sure is good to be outta that place," Amos said.

"We need to find the real culprit before your trial date," Michael reminded him as they walked toward his office.

"Amos, John and I can drive you home if you need a ride," Osi offered.

"I'd be much obliged. I knowed y'all's got lots to do with Gentle Woman laid up and all, but I'm gonna take you up on your offer. It's a mighty long ways to walk."

"I'll need to stop by Michael's house before we go," Osi told him. "I have a few things to discuss with Mother about Marietta Place."

"I think I'll let you take Amos home by yourself," John said. "By the time we get to the house, I'll be ready for my afternoon nap."

"That's fine," Osi assured him. "I'll see if Koi wants to go with me."

"When are you planning on heading back to Tishomingo?" Matthew asked.

John hesitated. "We haven't decided. It all depends. Gentle Woman will need to get her strength back. We'll be staying at the hotel until she's able to travel."

"I better get busy," Michael said when they all arrived at the law office. "I have my work cut out for me. I'll see y'all later this evening. I'm sure Violet will have dinner ready for us and will expect everyone to be there."

"Thanks. By the time I get back from taking Amos home, I'll be starved," Osi replied. He, John, and Amos then climbed into John's buggy and drove off.

"Let me off at the front door. I'm pretty tired," John

requested.

Osi let him out before taking the buggy to the stable. Ples was in the barn and Osi told him, "I've got to take Amos home. Would you please tend to the horse and buggy?"

"Yes, sir, right away, Mr. Nance." Ples took the reins when Osi stepped down.

"Amos, aren't you coming in the house with me?" Osi asked.

"No, you go ahead. I ain't presentable to be goin' in the McIvers' house," Amos said, knowing he was infested with lice.

"All right, I shouldn't be too long. Are you hungry?"

"You knows I can always eat."

"Okay, I'll bring you some food and you can eat it on the way." Osi left Ples and Amos to tend to the matter at hand. "Anybody home?" he shouted as he walked in the back door.

"We're in here," Koi said from the parlor. "You must have tired Father out. He went straight to his bedroom when he got in."

Osi walked over to his mother and patted her on the arm. "I'm glad you're doing better."

"I'm fine," Gentle Woman assured him. "Just a little weak, but I'm getting stronger by the minute."

"I have a few things I need to talk to you about," Osi said.

"I'll leave if this is private," Koi offered.

"No, you can stay. I just have a question about Marietta Place."

"What is it, Osi?" Gentle Woman asked.

"I know you have food in the cellar and smokehouse. What do you think about donating it to the Brooks family?"

"That sounds like a fine idea. We can't haul it back with us to Tishomingo without hiring a wagon. There're so many mouths to feed at the Brooks' place that I'm sure they will appreciate it."

"That's a wonderful idea!" Koi agreed.

"Koi, do you want to go with me to take Amos home? Michael bailed him out of jail a little while ago. He's waiting in the buggy."

"Yes, I'd love to. Give me a minute to change my clothes," Koi said and rushed out of the room.

Osi had no idea how his mother would react to hearing her property would be sold, and he couldn't figure out a way to gently tell her. He fidgeted in his seat before finally blurting out, "Mother, I went to the abstract office and put the property up for sale."

Gentle Woman took a deep breath. "I figured as much. There's not much else we can do," she sighed.

"I know moving back to the ranch will be an inconvenience for you after living at Marietta Place, but I'll do what I can to make you comfortable."

"That won't be necessary. John has asked me to move to Okla Chuka. The more I think about it, the better I like the idea. I'll get to spend time with my grandbaby."

Osi smiled. "Looks like I'll be making lots of trips back and forth between the ranch and Tishomingo."

Just then Koi rushed into the parlor. "Okay, I'm ready."

Osi stood to leave. "We'll be back before dark. Michael said Violet would be expecting us for supper. By the way, where is she?"

"I think she went to town. If you're wondering who's tending me, you needn't worry. Rose and Kash are here."

"All right then. We'll see you at supper."

Amos was still sitting in the buggy when Osi and Koi arrived at the barn. "You can get some food at Marietta Place," Osi told him. "I didn't want to take anything from Violet's kitchen without asking."

"I thought Marietta Place burnt down?"

"Not the cellar or the smokehouse."

Osi helped Koi into the backseat of the buggy before climbing into the driver's seat.

It was only a short ride across town to Marietta Place. When they arrived, Koi said, "This place holds a lot of memories. I remember how excited Gentle Woman was when she discovered there was a hand pump in the kitchen and she no longer had to carry buckets of water from the well." She became dewy-eyed when she saw Gentle Woman's metal swing still standing in the yard next to the rose garden. Not so long ago, Osi had placed it there so they could sit and watch fireflies, listen to the sound of crickets chirping, and enjoy each

39

other's company in the stillness of the night. It was a peaceful time back then, without all the complications of recent months.

"Amos, let's get started loading stuff up," Osi said, interrupting Koi's daydreams.

"What are we gonna load?"

"Food. Gentle Woman said to give it to y'all. We probably can't get it all in the buggy this trip, but next time you come to town with your wagon, you can come by and get the rest."

Koi hopped down, went directly to the smokehouse, and started carrying slabs of meat to the buggy. She wished that she had brought some rags, a blanket, or something to put over the meat to keep the flies and dirt from getting on it. Looking around, she spotted the lap robe neatly folded over the back of the buggy seat. She placed it on top of the meat.

Osi walked around where the house had once stood, kicking at the ashes. He was checking to see if there was anything that could be salvaged before going to the cellar. When he was satisfied there was nothing left of value, he walked away.

The cellar was several yards from the house and had not been touched by the fire, other than a layer of black soot covering the galvanized tin doors. One door was open when Osi walked up. He bent down and peered inside the earthy-smelling dugout. "Amos, you in there?"

There was no reply. When Osi stepped down into the cellar, he saw Amos sitting on a dirt bench, eating fruit and drinking from a quart jar. Osi couldn't help feeling pity for this poor ignorant soul.

Amos had peach juice running out both sides of his mouth and down the bib of his filthy overalls. "I do believe this is the best canned peaches I ever et," Amos uttered between swallows.

"Yep, my mother's a good cook. Let's get going though. The quicker we get this food loaded, the sooner we can get you home." Osi stepped inside the cellar. He immediately started looking around for a box to put the jars in and spotted a spliced-wood fruit basket. He picked it up and hit it against the wall to knock the spiders and dirt off before sitting it on the floor. "This ought to do," he said. He loaded the basket and carried it to the

40

buggy.

Amos helped himself to another jar of fruit before he picked up a few items to load.

◊◊◊

It didn't take long before the buggy was full. Koi had loaded the slabs of meat onto the back seat. Now she had nowhere to sit, so she crawled on top of the lap robe covering the meat for her ride to the Brooks' house.

"It'll take us longer to get to your house than I thought it would," Osi said. "This buggy is loaded to the brim."

When they finally approached the house, the guinea fowl signaled someone was coming with their obnoxious squawking. Before the buggy came to a halt, several children ran to greet their father.

Sally came out of the house and joined the children, walking alongside the slow-moving vehicle. "Amos, I see they done got you outta the jailhouse," she said, welcoming him home.

"Yeah, I hope I don't never have to go back there again."

Osi pulled the buggy to a halt. "We're going to have to hurry and get this food unloaded so we can get back on the road. We'll never make it before dark if we don't get a move on."

◊◊◊

Soon Osi and Koi were on the road back to Ardmore. They sat quietly as they rode along, but after a while Osi said, "My mother tells me you're going to live at Okla Chuka when we get back."

"Yes, Osi. You and I both know it would be the respectable thing to do."

"It might be, but it isn't what I want."

"Me, either, but for now we must live apart."

Osi pulled the buggy to a stop, jumped down, and went behind a tree alongside the roadway. Koi thought it was a nature call, but shortly he came back to the buggy and

41

presented her with a willow flower.

Koi was touched by his gift. He used to give her carved willow flowers every time he came to see her. By this gesture he was saying, *Will you be mine?*

He stepped into the buggy, leaned over, and put his arm around her. Then he pulled her close and kissed her passionately.

"Osi, we'll never make it back in time for supper."

"Who cares about supper when I have you," Osi whispered in her ear.

Lovemaking in the buggy proved to be too difficult, so Koi grabbed the lap robe and placed it on the ground.

◇◇◇

On the way back to town, Koi was quiet for a while. Then, to start a conversation, she said, "One of these days we'll remember this and laugh about making love at the side of the road."

Osi smiled. "I won't laugh. I'll think it was a great idea."

When they arrived at the McIver house, everyone was waiting for them. The men were smoking on the porch and the women were visiting in the parlor.

"Hi," Koi said, waving as she passed the parlor on the way to her bedroom. "Give me a minute to clean up and I'll be in to see y'all."

She was happy to see Jennie with Gentle Woman and Violet. Violet was cooing over Jacob, and Gentle Woman was trying to corral Kash. It was almost time to call Rose to come get the children. She would be tending them tonight so the families could dine without disruption.

Koi knew Mrs. McIver didn't entertain very often and had gone all out for this evening's meal. She had extended the dining table with extra leaves to make it large enough for everyone to be seated comfortably. She was using her best tablecloth and had set the table formally with the bone china she had brought from Louisiana.

By the time Koi walked into the dining room, everyone

else was seated. The men pushed their chairs back and stood while John pulled a chair out for his daughter to sit next to him. "Sorry it took me so long," Koi apologized.

"No problem. You look like my little Indian girl tonight in your calico dress," John said, beaming with pride.

"Osi tells me this dress is his favorite," Koi winked.

"John, would you do us the honor of saying the blessing?" Michael asked.

"I'd be proud to oblige."

After the prayer, a platter of baked ham, along with several serving dishes loaded with sweet potatoes, green beans, wild onions, pickled okra, and a pitcher of redeye gravy were circulated around the table.

"Violet, you've prepared a meal fit for royalty," John exclaimed.

"I'll agree to that," Osi echoed. "Everything is delicious."

Koi and Jennie started a polite conversation while Gentle Woman and Violet sat, quietly eating their food.

"I had a couple of interesting visitors today," Michael said, breaking the silence.

"Anyone we might know?" John asked.

"You don't know them, but you would recognize them as the representatives from the office of Indian Affairs. We saw them in the courtroom when we were in Chicago. They're in town, investigating the Syndicate. They came to my office in smart-looking suits, and I told 'em if they didn't want to stand out like sore thumbs, they better go buy themselves jeans and cowboy boots."

"The minute they stepped off the train, word probably spread like wildfire that strangers are in town," Matthew said. "They didn't seem a bit surprised when I told 'em Francis Kirby had been killed and the murder had been blamed on a poor pathetic squaw man."

"I'm glad to see the Commissioner of Indian Affairs has made good on his promise to send them here. It's about time," Osi said.

"I'm sure we'll be seeing more of them. It'll be interesting to find out what they come up with," John replied.

After the evening meal, Michael invited the men to

43

continue their conversation with an after-dinner smoke on the porch while the women retired to the parlor.

"Are you ready for bed?" Violet asked Gentle Woman a short time later.

"Yes. I'll say goodnight and thank you for a wonderful meal and pleasant evening with family and friends."

"I'll walk you to your bedroom, Mother, if you want me to," Koi offered.

"That's my job," Violet smiled.

Before long everybody announced they were ready to turn in. John's family said their goodbyes before leaving to go to the hotel. After this long and eventful day, they were all looking forward to a good night's sleep.

Chapter Six

They had a long road ahead of them, so early the next morning the family expressed their appreciation to the McIvers for their generosity and were quickly on their way to Tishomingo. Before leaving, though, John and Osi assured Michael and Matthew they would search for clues pertaining to the murder of Francis Kirby and would be in touch soon.

◊◊◊

"I have my work cut out for me," Osi said when they approached his ranch. "I hope the wranglers have taken better care of the fences and livestock than they have this overgrown yard." He stepped down from the buggy. "Y'all have a safe trip and I'll be seeing you as soon as I can get the ranch in order." He gave Koi and his mother a peck on the cheek, patted Kash on the top of his head, shook John's hand, and then waved goodbye as the family continued along the road to Tishomingo.

To his dismay, much had been neglected in his absence. At dawn the next day, Osi and the wranglers wasted no time starting to mend fences, brand cattle, and cull livestock to take to market in the spring. Osi was determined to get the ranch running smoothly once again. Then he would go to Okla Chuka to see Koi and Kash.

◊◊◊

The Pritchetts and Gentle Woman arrived at Okla Chuka to find a layer of dust covering everything in the house. One thing about the Territory, it had plenty of red dirt, and it found its way inside every room of the house. Insects buzzed around them, and Koi swatted at the pests while she set to work dusting a clean spot on the parlor sofa to lay Kash. He was sound asleep and she hoped he would stay that way long enough for her to get his bed prepared.

When John opened the door to the great room, a stale tobacco odor spilled out, bringing back memories of bygone days. It struck him as painfully eerie. This room was where he had smoked and greeted visitors throughout the years. He remembered entertaining Neville the night he arrived in the Territory. Now spider webs connected the furniture to the wall hangings.

His eyes were drawn to the many sentimental decorations adorning the room: deerskins, a feathered war bonnet, and a ceremonial peace pipe. They were now covered with powdery red dirt. The mounted buffalo head over the fireplace mantle seemed to be staring at him through a film of grime. The deer head hat rack next to the door still had John's overcoat draped over one of the antlers. On the floor in front of the fireplace was the black panther skin Osi and Koi had napped on as youngsters. John couldn't bear to see his favorite room in such a mess. He closed the door, shutting away his emotions, and walked down the hall to his bedroom.

Koi found her room sealed with cobwebs. She took a broomstick, tied a piece of muslin on one end, and used it to knock down the spider webs before opening the door. She meticulously inspected and cleaned Kash's bed before moving him.

The next morning Koi awoke itching and scratching. "Rose, the cups around the bedposts need filling with coal oil. I think we might have acquired some bed bugs while we were gone."

"Yes, ma'am. I'll get to it right away," Rose said as she tired to scurry past John in the hall.

John held out a hand to stop her. "You've been working

non-stop," he remarked.

"The work won't get done by itself." Rose wiped her brow as she hustled to get the kerosene.

John realized she was having a hard time keeping up. He walked to the back door and held it open for her. "Rose, do you know of anyone who might be interested in working here? I think we need to get someone to assist you with the daily chores."

"I'd be much obliged, Mr. Prichett, for any extra help I can get. My cousin's daughter, Stevetta, might want to work here."

"I'll go to town this afternoon and find out," John said, letting the screen door slam shut.

John returned from Tishomingo late that afternoon, bringing with him a Negro girl who appeared to be in her early twenties. He drove the buggy directly to the stable and handed the reins to Ples. "Ples, this is Stevetta. She's Rose's kinfolk. She'll be working for us now." He walked in the back door and headed straight for the great room. "Rose?" he yelled. "Stevetta is out back with Ples. Better get a room ready for her."

Hearing John's words, Rose hurried to greet Stevetta. "My goodness gracious, how you've growed since I last saw you," Rose said, eyeing the young woman from head to toe. "You's a fine young lady now. Give your kin a big hug and then we can bring your trunk into the house and I'll show you what needs to be done."

For the next few days, Stevetta scrubbed floors and emptied the chamber pots while Rose washed clothes and managed the kitchen. They worked diligently, making the house look like it had a few months ago, before the family left for Chicago.

Koi spent most of her time with Kash. He was at an age that demanded constant attention. Very seldom did she have time to draw, write in her journal, or play her piano. Most afternoons were spent taking Kash for horseback rides along the banks of Pennington Creek on Koi's horse, Cricket, who was slow and gentle.

47

Koi missed Osi and often thought of him, especially when she passed the waterfall. "Kash, see that big whirlpool?" Koi pointed to the spot. She knew he was too young to understand what she was saying, but she wanted to start warning him early about the danger of the swirling water. "That's a no-no. You should never go there, it's dangerous."

Looking at the cascading water, Koi's mind rushed back to the day she and Osi had ventured into the cave behind the waterfall. They had been warned as youngsters to stay away from this forbidden place, but the temptation to explore had pulled them like a magnet. She remembered the thrill and excitement of danger as they carefully climbed over huge wet boulders. They had inched their way along the edge of the rocks, slipping, sliding, and praying they wouldn't fall. After reaching the cavern behind the misty veil of water, Osi had laughed and collapsed on the moist earth. Before Koi had time to catch her breath, he'd pulled her down beside him and they had slowly melted into each other on the mossy blanket covering the floor of the cave.

Koi sighed, thinking about those carefree days with Osi. Her thoughts were interrupted when Kash dropped the reins and she had to get off Cricket to retrieve them.

"Here, Kash. Hold onto the saddle horn," she said, placing his tiny hands around the pommel. She decided to walk rather than ride back to Okla Chuka. She had much to think about. The idea of opening a school of art and music for children in Tishomingo kept crossing her mind.

◊◊◊

One afternoon Koi and Gentle Woman were sitting on the porch swing, watching Kash play in the yard, when John walked out the front door. "How about us having a party soon?" he suggested. "I need to catch up on what's been happening around here. I might be able to find something out about the mystery surrounding Francis Kirby's murder."

"That's a great idea," Koi replied before rushing to prevent Kash from getting into a sticker bush. "Osi will be here, won't he?" she asked.

"He'll be the first on the guest list. I know he's as curious as I am to find out who did it."

For the next two weeks, everyone at Okla Chuka prepared for the party. John sent invitations to several respected leaders of the Chickasaw Nation, along with a few businessmen from town, asking them to join the family for this gala event. He contemplated over whether or not to invite the Jacksons but finally decided they might have some clue about Francis Kirby's murder, so he put their names on the guest list.

Luther Jackson, Jennie McIver's brother, was Governor of the Chickasaw Nation. John and Osi, both National Party members, didn't have much to do with Luther or his father, George, since they were staunch members of the Progressive Party.

Tension had grown stronger between the political factions ever since the Jacksons had called for a recount of votes in the governor's election. To make matters worse, Matthew McIver, a National Party member, had married Jennie Jackson. John hoped everyone would be cordial, and he prayed that the evening would not end in an altercation.

The former governor, Smith Reynolds, and his wife replied to the invitation with an apology, saying they couldn't make it due to prior commitments. Michael McIver, his wife, Violet, and their son, Matthew, confirmed their invitation.

Jennie regretfully informed Koi that she wouldn't be making the trip to Okla Chuka until baby Jacob was a little older. Koi was disappointed, but she was busy getting ready for the formal dinner, and it was a relief to have one less thing to be concerned about. She would see Jennie another time, when they could spend quality time together.

The day before the big event, Koi was sitting on the porch, writing in her journal, when she looked up to see Osi riding toward the house on Koiishto Losa. She remembered him telling her why he had given his horse the name Black Panther. "He has a coat as slick and black as a panther," he'd said.

Koi felt her emotions rise when she saw Osi. In the pit of her stomach, she had a tickling sensation that reminded her of a thousand butterflies flapping their wings. Her heart pounded so loudly she could hear it thumping inside her chest.

Osi reined his horse to a stop near the hitching post, ran up the steps, and swept her into his arms. "I've missed you," he whispered. He brushed her hair from her face and nibbled at her ear. Before Koi had time to respond, they heard the front door open and quickly released their embrace.

"I thought I heard someone riding up," John said, stepping out onto the porch. "Come on in and get something to drink."

"I'll take you up on that offer," Osi replied. "Lemonade sounds pretty good right now." He turned and winked at Koi as he walked into the house behind John.

"Rose? Stevetta?" John shouted. "Bring us some lemonade. We'll be in the great room."

"How's Mother?" Osi asked as he and John took their favorite seats.

"She's doing fine. I'm sure she'll be in here to see you when she knows you've arrived. How about a smoke?" John offered Osi a cigar.

"Don't mind if I do," Osi said, choosing one with the sweet scent of cherries. "You must've restocked your supply, from the looks of your overflowing humidor."

"Yep. We're expecting a lot of people here tomorrow night. I wanted to make sure to have enough." John sat back in his chair and lit up his cigar. "I'm glad you came early. You can help Ples and me get some last minute details done."

"I'll be glad to help. Just point me in the right direction and tell me what you need. But from the looks of it, you seem to have everything under control."

"Pretty much, thanks to Rose and Stevetta."

Koi, carrying Kash, peeked into the great room. "Are you two busy?" she asked. "I'd like to show Osi how much Kash has grown in a month." Koi stood Kash on the floor and he immediately walked to John's chair.

John picked him up and said, "Give Papaw a kiss, big boy."

Kash puckered up and planted a wet one on John's cheek.

Koi watched Osi's reaction at seeing Kash and her

50

father's interaction. She could tell by the way he stared at them that he was a bit envious of their bond. She went to her father, took Kash from his arms, and walked to where Osi was sitting. "Would you like to hold him?" she asked.

Osi squirmed in his seat. "He really doesn't know me and I don't want to scare him." He cracked a nervous smile.

Koi turned to Kash. "Kash, this is Osi. Can you say Osi?"

"See," he tried to mimic her.

"That's good. Try again. *Oh see*," she said slowly.

Kash's voice plainly erupted with, "Oh see."

"Yes! That's right!" Koi turned proudly to John and Osi. "He's learning to talk so quickly. He says a new word almost every day." She stood Kash on the floor in front of Osi, hoping he would pick him up.

Osi smiled and gently patted the top of Kash's head. "It won't be long until he will be out-talking us."

Koi wanted Kash and Osi to bond, but she wasn't going to push too fast. She grinned, knowing this was the first baby step in that direction. "It's time Kash and I go see what Rose and Stevetta are cooking for dinner." She scooped the baby into her arms and walked out of the room.

After supper the family retired early, leaving Osi and Koi to spend time alone. They sat on the porch, enjoying the stillness of the evening until a cool breeze caused them to go inside. Koi walked into the great room, sat down on the panther rug in front of the fireplace, and warmed her toes on the hearth. Without saying a word, Osi pulled her to him and held her close to his heart as they went to sleep.

◊◊◊

Everyone was up bright and early the next morning. The entire day was spent getting the final preparations done and by late afternoon everything was ready for the big event. As the sun gilded the treetops and danced along the crest of the rolling hills west of Tishomingo, the guests made their way up the road to Okla Chuka.

Koi wore an elegant, lace-trimmed, blue brocade dress

51

with tiny pink roses embroidered on the bodice. She had piled her hair into a loose coiffure on top of her head, leaving a few strands to fall on her shoulders. Once she was dressed, she went into the parlor and began playing the piano. Osi spotted her and came to join in. He wore a brown suit cut in the latest fashion. Koi recognized it as the suit he had worn at his trial in Chicago. This night they could have passed for upper-crust socialites from Chicago or New York.

"Koi, play my favorite song," Osi requested.

She looked down to avoid showing her longing for him and began to play "Beautiful Dreamer."

Before the song was over, Osi heard John calling. "Osi, come into the great room. I'd like you to greet the men when they come into the house. I'll be on the porch welcoming guests as they arrive." Koi's heart fluttered as she watched Osi walk out of the room with her father.

Rose brought Kash into the parlor and sat him near the piano to play with his blocks. "Miz Koi, I put his Sunday best clothes on him. Does he look presentable to you?"

"You did a good job, Rose. He looks very nice," Koi said.

"If you don't mind, I think I better get outta these work clothes and into my maid's uniform before the guests arrive."

"Of course, run ahead. Kash will be just fine right here."

◊◊◊

Ples and two stableboys stood outside the picket fence, waiting to take the horses and buggies to the barn. Before long several people could be seen coming up the long drive. John and Gentle Woman welcomed each person as they stepped onto the porch. Most of the guests spoke English, so they were greeted with, "Welcome to Okla Chuka." However, John and Gentle Woman knew which fullbloods preferred the Chickasaw language and greeted them with, "*Chokma.*"

Times were changing rapidly in the Territory, and by now most Chickasaw men could speak English, although they preferred their own language. The only person at the party who didn't speak or understand English was Moses Creek. Moses was a respected elder and the only Chickasaw citizen who could vividly remember the long trek, sixty-plus years ago, from Mississippi to their new homeland in Indian Territory.

The last time Moses visited Okla Chuka for a dinner party was a few years ago when Koi's mother, Carrie, was still alive. Moses had been fond of Carrie. They'd had a special way of communicating without speaking, since neither knew the other's language. Moses had been morose when Carrie passed and had shed sorrowful tears at her funeral.

◊◊◊

John ushered the men into the great room for a smoke. He smiled when he noticed Simon Rabbit wearing the same suit with the stiff celluloid collar and tie he had worn the last time he had come to Okla Chuka.

Gentle Woman escorted the women into the parlor to be entertained by Koi playing the piano. When she heard the McIvers arriving, she went to greet them. "Come on in, Violet," she said, ushering her into the room.

"I am so glad to see you doing well," Violet whispered, not wanting to disrupt Koi's song. She took a seat next to Gentle Woman to enjoy the rest of the entertainment.

After about half an hour, Rose and Stevetta lit tapers in the silver candelabra on the banquet table and opened the dining room doors to let the guests know that dinner would now be served. The guests quickly poured into the dining area from both the parlor and the great room.

Koi had prepared the seating arrangements by putting delicately painted place cards next to the plates. Her father's seat was at the head of the table. She knew John would want to be near Michael and Matthew, so she put their name cards on either side of him. Violet's place was next to Michael. Koi, with Kash in his high chair, sat across from Osi and Gentle Woman. Koi had purposefully placed Luther and George Jackson at the far end of the table, keeping them away from her father, Osi, and the McIvers. She wanted to avoid any heated discussion over politics at this social gathering. The rest of the name cards were placed at random, filling the lengthy table.

John said grace before Rose, Stevetta, and Ples started passing the serving plates around the table. They made sure everyone received all the food they wanted. Some of the fullbloods ate with their fingers rather than with the silverware. No one seemed to notice or care, since they were accustomed to seeing them eat their food this way.

Polite niceties and small talk continued until John stood, tapped his water glass with a spoon, and spoke loudly enough for everyone to hear. "I planned this dinner party so we could come together as friends and community members to discuss the bad dealings we've been having with outsiders coming to the Territory and cheating us out of land and money. Many of you already know my family hasn't gone untouched. We've had the wool pulled over our eyes by one such devious character. I won't embarrass my daughter by mentioning his name, but he is no longer part of this family nor is he alive to continue his conniving schemes." An awkward silence filled the room.

Koi was shocked her father had brought up the subject of her late husband. Her face flushed red with embarrassment.

John continued. "As you know, Francis Kirby, the banker, was found murdered a few weeks ago. One of our galvanized citizens, Amos Brooks, was arrested for the murder. We all know poor old Amos didn't do it. If anyone here has any clues as to who might have had something to do with the murder, please tell us." John nodded to Michael and Matthew. "The Commissioner of Indian Affairs from Washington, D.C., has sent two investigators to ferret out the bunch responsible for stealing our land. They didn't expect to walk right into a murder mystery. The McIvers' law firm is working with them to find the culprit and clear Amos's name. If you know anything, please tell us. With your help we may be able to rid our nation of these thieves."

Osi sat quietly during the meal, observing the guests. He noticed everyone except the Jacksons gave their full attention to John. Luther and George continued to eat when the others clapped and cheered politely after John's speech.

Before sitting back down in his chair, John gleefully smiled. "Let's celebrate this evening with good friends and family by having some grape dumplings for dessert."

Chapter Seven

After breakfast the men retired to the great room. Drawing on a newly lit cigar from the humidor, Michael took a puff and slowly blew out the smoke. "Matthew and I have decided to open a law office in Tishomingo."

"Sounds like a great idea to me," John smiled. "Tishomingo needs a good lawyer, and we'd get to see you more often. This town is growing. There's a lot of new construction on Main Street. And it looks like we're going to get some culture here in the Territory before long. An opera house is being built."

Before John had time to say anything else, Osi asked Matthew, "Does that mean y'all would be moving here full time?"

Matthew cleared his throat, "Yes. Jennie, Jacob, and I will be making Tishomingo our home. I'll open the office in Tishomingo and Dad will run the one in Ardmore.

"Koi's going to be thrilled. When are you planning on making the move?" Osi asked.

"I thought we could look for potential office space today," Matthew said. "If we find something suitable, I'll get home and start packing."

John snuffed out his cigar. "A new, two-story, red brick building is going up where the old Farmers National Bank used to be. I don't know if it's completed yet, but we can go to town and see. One of the men at the party last night mentioned it's going to be another bank building. They might have space available. Let's go as soon as Ples gets the buggy ready."

◊◊◊

After breakfast Violet and Gentle Woman retired to the parlor to work on their needlework projects. Gentle Woman, still recuperating from the fire, spent her days crocheting, and Violet was working on a pair of knitted booties for Jacob. Before the women picked up their work, Violet was already telling Gentle Woman all about her little grandson. "You know, he looks just like Matthew, except for his dark skin."

◇◇◇

When the men walked outside, Koi and Kash were on the porch. "Koi, we're going to town for the day," John announced. "I don't know what time we'll be back, but it'll be before supper. Tell Rose and Stevetta we'll be having our noon meal downtown."

"All right, Father," Koi said meekly. She was disappointed because she had been hoping to spend time with Osi, but it appeared that her father would be keeping him occupied.

As Osi stepped off the porch behind the other men, he turned and gave Koi a wink and a nod. Her heart never failed to skip a beat when he looked at her that way. She hoped he would stay at Okla Chuka a few days longer than the others so they could talk.

◇◇◇

The sun was going down by the time the men returned. They drove directly to the stable and handed the horse and buggy over to Ples.

"We're home," John yelled as he stepped inside the back door.

Mrs. McIver walked out of the parlor to greet them. "Did you find a place?"

"We sure did," Matthew said. "We put a deposit down and can move in next month."

"Looks like your father and I will be left alone in Ardmore," Violet said sadly, realizing she wouldn't get to see her grandbaby as often as she liked.

Gentle Woman was now at Mrs. McIver's side. She put

56

her arm around Violet. "You know you're welcome to come here anytime you want," she assured her friend. Addressing the men, she said, "You better get cleaned up, Rose and Stevetta have dinner almost ready." Then she turned to John. "If you have a minute, I need to talk to you in private."

"Sure, let's go into the great room."

After they took seats next to each other, Gentle Woman stared directly at John with a serious look on her face. "I, uh," she stumbled over her words, "I-I didn't want to say anything in front of the others, but, uh, the privy is overflowing. We had so many guests here at the dinner party, they filled it to the brim, and I think it's time to call the scavenger man to come clean up the mess."

John tried to hold back the chuckle that suddenly erupted in the back of his throat. He coughed to keep from bursting out with laughter. "I'm glad you told me. I'll make sure Ples gets someone out here right away to take care of it. Thank you." He rose to his feet and was still smiling as he walked away.

After dinner when everyone went out to the porch to enjoy the evening, Michael announced, "We'll be heading back to Ardmore in the morning. It sure has been a nice visit. The more time I spend in Tishomingo, the better I like it. Maybe one of these days, when I retire, Violet and I might decide to move here."

Violet perked up. "Michael, I'm ready to move right now. It's going to be hard not seeing Jacob every day."

Koi jumped in. "Mrs. McIver, I'd love it if your entire family moved to Tish'. I'm thrilled Jennie and I will be raising our boys together."

John, Gentle Woman, and the McIvers continued with small talk about Matthew opening a law office in Tishomingo. Koi and Osi sat quietly on the porch swing with Kash between them. The rhythmic, back and forth movement rocked him to sleep and his head slumped over to rest on Osi's arm. Osi sat for a few moments, not knowing what to do. Finally, he eased his arm up and placed it around Kash, cuddling him close.

"Koi, would you like for me to carry him to bed?"

"Sure," she agreed. She was pleased he was taking an interest in their son.

Osi carefully lifted Kash without waking him and slowly walked to the door. Koi rushed to open it and they walked to her room. She rolled back the covers on Kash's bed and Osi tenderly laid him down, slowly draping the coverlet over the tiny body. He turned, pulled Koi to him, and looked lovingly into her eyes. "We made a beautiful son, didn't we?" Osi drew her closer, brushed the wayward strands of hair from her face and nibbled at her neck, working his way to her lips.

"Osi, not here, not now," Koi whispered.

"I know," Osi sighed as he planted another kiss on her lips. "Would you like to go on a picnic tomorrow?"

"Yes, it would be like old times," Koi grinned happily. She took his hand and led him out of the room and back onto the porch.

Early the next morning the McIvers waved goodbye as they headed back to Ardmore. Koi was so excited about going on a picnic with Osi that she had hardly slept a wink all night. After breakfast she followed Rose to the kitchen and prepared a basket of food for the outing.

"Rose, I hope Kash won't be a problem for you today while I am gone," Koi said.

"Miz Koi, I'm sure he'll be just fine. I thought I'd take him outdoors in the garden with me and give him a spoon to dig in the dirt. That should keep him busy for a while."

"I'm sure he would love that." Koi smiled. "Father said the scavenger man would be coming today to clean out the outhouse. When he shows up, be sure to bring Kash inside."

"Yes, ma'am, I'll surely do that. It's gonna smell bad around here for a while," Rose replied.

Osi and John turned their horses into the stable after making the morning rounds to check on the livestock. "I don't see Ples," Osi said.

"He's probably in town, fetching the scavenger man. I told him last night to go get someone to clean out the privy right away." John smiled as he thought of how Gentle Woman had acted when she mentioned it was overflowing. "Your mother was a bit embarrassed when she told me it needed tending to."

Osi didn't reply. He simply grinned.

They took care of their horses and put their saddles away.

"Koi and I are going on a picnic today," Osi said.

"Looks like it's going to be a nice day," John replied. "Maybe it would be a good time to talk about when y'all want to get married."

"I'd like to tie the knot right away, but Koi has to be the one to say when."

John nodded. "I know she's afraid of what people might think if she marries too soon after Neville's death, but I say who cares what they think."

"My sentiments exactly," Osi agreed as he hitched Bess up to the small buggy and drove it to the front of the house. "Koi, you ready?" Osi shouted.

"Just about. Here, take, this basket," she said, handing Osi the wickerwork container. "I'll run get a tablecloth to spread on the ground and be right back."

Osi stowed the basket behind the seat and waited for Koi to come out of the house so he could help her into the buggy. Soon they were on their way down the long drive and toward the creek.

◊◊◊

Around noon Ples came home with the scavenger man. The man drove his team of mules and flatbed wagon as close to the outhouse as he could then he and Ples struggled to move the wooden structure away from the pit.

"There you go. The rest is up to you." Ples brushed his hands together, trying to knock off any dirt. "I'll either be in the stable or the barn. Let me know when you're ready to leave so I can get Mr. Prichett to pay you." Ples pulled a handkerchief from his pocket and held it over his nose as he rushed to the house.

Rose opened the door with Kash on her hip when Ples knocked loudly. "What's the matter, Ples? You got a nose bleed?" she asked.

"No. I just came to warn y'all to close all the windows, 'cause the scavenger man is here cleanin' the outhouse and it don't smell good."

Rose slammed the door and ran to button up the house. "Stevetta," she yelled. "There'll be no hangin' clothes on the line today. We best find things to do inside the house."

◊◊◊

"Osi, can we have our picnic at Mill Pond?" Koi asked.

"Sure, but I thought you might like to go to the waterfall," Osi replied.

"I'd rather not, if you don't mind. I know a perfect boulder we can sit on and the water is quieter at Mill Pond."

"That sounds good to me, but how about taking a little ride around town before going to the creek."

"Oh, I'd like that," Koi smiled. "Will you show me Matthew's new office?"

"We can drive by the building, but it'd be best if we don't disturb the workers." When they arrived at the corner of Main and Kemp, Osi told her, "See that two-story building? Matthew's office will be located on the second floor. His name will be the first one you see at the top of the stairs." Osi continued to drive along Main Street, pointing out several new buildings.

It was late in the afternoon before Osi stopped the buggy near the creek. "I'll tie the horse here and we can walk the rest of the way," he said, pulling the buggy close to a large pecan tree. He helped Koi from the buggy and then lifted the picnic basket from the back. "I don't know if any snakes are out yet, but you better let me walk in front of you, just in case," he warned.

Koi felt safe with Osi. He could smell a snake long before he ever saw one. Many times when they'd been teenagers he would clear an area along the creek of snakes before letting her swim. Osi said that water moccasins have a musty smell with a faint hint of skunk. As hard as she tried, she never could smell one.

Before long she pointed to a large, protruding boulder. "There's the spot I had in mind."

Osi lead the way down the steep creek bank and up onto the large granite rock. He set the basket down and reached his hand to help Koi up.

"I love this creek so much. I can't imagine living anywhere but here," Koi said.

"When I was in the Chicago jail, I wanted a drink of water from here so bad. There's no other place in the world that has water this good. There's something about it that tastes like none other." Osi grinned and pulled her to him.

◊◊◊

All afternoon the scavenger man continued to shovel waste onto the back of his wagon. Soon it was a large heaping pile. Out of curiosity John opened the door a crack to peek. He wanted to see how much *yalhki* had been extracted. The stench caused him to quickly close the door.

The pit was almost cleaned out when the man made one last shovel thrust to the bottom of the hole. It clinked on something metal. He dug a little deeper and was able to retrieve a metal object. He dumped the shovel load onto the ground and was shocked to see a gun covered in feces jutting out from the offal. He took off running as fast as he could toward the barn. "Ples, where are you?" he yelled.

Ples looked around a stall to see the filthy man running toward him. "What's going on?"

"I found a gun," the scavenger man said.

Ples ran to the house, yelling for John. "Mr. Prichett! Come quick!"

John came to the door to find Ples in a state of panic. "What's the matter?"

"A gun was found in the bottom of the pit!"

"Wonder who threw it in there?" John asked as they

hurried to the site. "Ples, go get a shovel and pick this thing up. Put it in a box and take it to the barn until I can take care of it." He walked back to the house, wondering how a gun had ended up in his outhouse. For now, he would do nothing but wait for Osi to return from his picnic.

The scavenger man continued his dirty job by putting lime in the pit, and then he asked Ples to help him scoot the little hut back over the hole.

"I'll go get your money," Ples said, once the task had been completed.

Soon the scavenger man and his wagonload of waste left Okla Chuka, dripping liquid all along the road.

Chapter Eight

Koi spread the tablecloth on a shady spot on the boulder and began removing food from the basket. "I'm so happy that Jennie and Matthew are going to be living here in Tishomingo."

"Yes, it'll be nice to have them close by," Osi said then he surprised her by saying, "Wait here. I'll be back in a minute." He stepped off the rock and went to a thicket of trees where he broke off a branch and began carving a willow flower.

A few minutes later, Koi yelled, "Osi, come quick!"

He dropped the branch and ran to where she stood pointing at something floating in the creek. They both stared in disbelief as they watched a half-submerged body drift along with the current.

"Oh, no!" Koi clutched her chest.

Without hesitation Osi jumped from the boulder and rushed to the edge of the water. "Go get your father. I'll need help pulling him out."

Koi scampered off the rock and ran as fast as she could to the buggy. She jumped in the seat and snapped the loose ends of the leather reins above Bess's head, which caused the horse to take off at a run.

When Koi passed the scavenger man's wagon on the road, she held her breath until it was far behind her. In a few minutes she stopped the buggy near the steps of the house and ran to the door. "Father, come quick!"

A startled John rushed from the great room. "What's going on?"

Koi tried to catch her breath. "We found a dead body floating in the creek."

"What! Who is it?"

"We don't know. Osi told me to come get you to help him pull the body out of the water."

"You stay here. I'll get Ples and we'll take the wagon. Where along the creek?" John asked as he hurried out the door.

"The big boulder at Mill Pond!" Koi yelled.

Hearing excited voices, Gentle Woman rushed to Koi's side. She put her arm around her and ushered her to a chair in the parlor. Koi fidgeted in her seat, wringing her hands. Then she clenched her skirt to sooth her nerves.

Gentle Woman took her hand. "Tell me what happened."

"We saw a body in the creek. It was turned face down and it kept bobbing up and down with the current. At first I thought it was a log, but when I saw blue cloth, I realized what it was."

Rose came into the parlor with Kash on her hip. "Your big boy just woke up from a nap," she said, breaking the somber mood.

Koi squeezed Kash tightly and gave him several kisses on the neck. "I hope he behaved himself today."

"He was a perfect little man, Miz Koi. The scavenger man was here so we had to stay indoors, but I kept him busy playing with his toys."

After another hug, Koi said, "I need you to watch him a little longer while I put Bess and buggy away. The men should be arriving shortly. Osi will probably be hungry since we didn't eat." Outside, Koi unhooked Bess and led her to a stall where she gave her feed and water. She took her time in the barn; she needed to be alone to calm her nerves.

◊◊◊

It was almost dark when the men came through the gates. Koi was in the kitchen giving Kash his supper when she heard the wagon pull up to the barn. "Rose, come finish feeding Kash," she called as she ran out the back door.

"Stay back." Osi held up his hand. "It's not a pretty picture."

Koi stood at a distance and watched the men struggle to

lift the bloated body from the back of the wagon and carry it inside the barn.

"Let's put him in one of the stalls," John suggested. They laid the body on fresh straw and covered it with a horse blanket.

Osi wrinkled his brow. "I can't believe it's Bois d'Arc. There's no way anyone should have been able to sneak up him. Shouldn't we be taking him home?"

John wiped his hands on his trousers. "Ordinarily, we would, but we can't take him home until we let the investigators see the wound on his head. It might be important to their investigation. In the meantime, we need to get him in a box."

Knowing Bois d'Arc's family was poor, John pulled a leather pouch from his pocket and handed Ples several coins. "First thing in the morning, I want you to take the wagon to Fillmore and buy a casket from the Chaney's. Isaac should have some for sale. Make sure you get one big enough, Bois d'Arc's body is pretty swollen."

John and Osi walked toward the house. Before they reached Koi, John tilted his head and yelled, "Ples, be sure to take plenty of straw with you tomorrow to cover the casket. I don't want people to see it before I notify the investigators."

Osi held the kitchen door open for Koi.

"Did you recognize who it was?" she asked.

"Yes, it's Bois d'Arc," he said.

"I wonder why he drowned? Everyone around here knows how to swim."

"Koi, he didn't drown," Osi said.

◊◊◊

Stevetta served supper while Rose tended Kash.

"You'd think I would be hungry, but I've lost my appetite," Koi said, moving her food around on her plate with her fork.

"Well, you better eat something," Gentle Woman told her. The men sat quietly, scarfing down their food, until John spoke. "His face is almost unrecognizable."

"That bullet hole in his head looked pretty nasty," Osi nodded.

Gentle Woman scowled. "Do you men have to talk about this at the supper table?"

John continued as if the women weren't in the room. "I can't figure out why someone would want to kill Bois d'Arc. We know he didn't have anything to do with the Syndicate. He was a Pull-Back, a member of the National Party, like us."

"Maybe he knew too much about the Syndicate and they needed him gone," Osi said as he sat his fork down. "I'll get the gun from the barn in the morning and wash it off so we can see what caliber it is.

The next day John sent a telegram to the McIvers. They were working closely with the investigators in Ardmore, and John knew the McIvers would know how to contact them. He was careful with his wording in the message. He didn't want Bois d'Arc's family to know about his death until the inspectors had finished examining his body. Afterwards, he and Osi would take him home.

While John was at the telegraph office, Osi went to retrieve the gun from the barn. He had to search several stalls before he found where Ples had hidden it. When he opened the box and saw it was encrusted with hardened feces, he quickly closed the lid and went in search of a bucket.

Osi turned away when he looked into one of the stalls and saw Bois d'Arc's body. His heart squeezed painfully, not only for Bois d'Arc but for his wife, Lawa, and their family. He found a slop bucket, carried it to the box, dumped the gun in the pail, and took it to the pump to fill with water. "I better let this soak a while," he said aloud.

Osi walked to the house and found Koi on the porch, writing in her journal. "What are you scribbling?"

Koi looked up. "I'm jotting down notes about a school for art and music I want to open one day for the children of the Chickasaw Nation."

"Where are you thinking of putting this school?" Osi asked, taking a seat on the steps.

"I'm going to talk to Father and see if he's agreeable to building a schoolroom right here at Okla Chuka."

Osi smiled. "I think a school for the arts is needed here in the Territory, and there wouldn't be a teacher anywhere better than you."

Koi sat her journal on the swing and went to him. He stood, pulled her close, and gave her a bear hug, lifting her off her feet. He swung her around before setting her down. "Let's get the buggy and go for a ride," he said.

Koi's eyes lit up. "Give me a few minutes to get ready." They drove into town and rode along Main Street, waving at people they knew and discussing how fast Tishomingo was growing. They soon drove passed the Methodist Church Koi and her mother had attended. Koi hadn't been to church since the new full-time pastor had been hired. "Osi, I think it's time I start taking Kash to Sunday school. He's getting old enough to start being around other children and learning Bible stories."

"Yes, I agree," Osi said. He turned the buggy around and drove south out of town.

"Are we going to Lookout Mound?" Koi asked.

Lookout Mound was a large outcropping of rocks and dirt, higher than most places in the area. It was south of Tishomingo and was steeped with legends of an earlier tribe of Indians who lived there long before the Chickasaws arrived. There was a spot on the south edge where one could see the valley below, and on a clear day the outline of Fort Washita was visible. In the past Osi had often taken Koi there when they wanted to be alone.

"Yes, we can lay in the grass and play the imaginary game of 'What do you see in the clouds,' like we used to when we were youngsters. If you want," Osi said grinning.

Playfully, Koi reached over and planted a kiss on his cheek.

67

◇◇◇

Two men dressed in black rode up the drive to Okla Chuka. They tied their horses to the hitching post, walked up the steps, and knocked on the door.

Stevetta opened it. "Hello, sirs. May I help you?"

The men opened their jackets at the same time to show their badges. "We're here representing the Commission of Indian Affairs, and we'd like to speak to Mr. John Prichett, please," the taller one said.

"I'll see if Mista Prichett is acceptin' company." Stevetta closed the door on them and went to find John. He was in the great room. "Mista Prichett, sir, there's some lawmen at the door askin' to talk to you."

"Show them in, Stevetta." John stood as she brought the men into the great room. He held out his hand and offered a friendly handshake. "Please, come, have a seat," John pointed to two chairs. "I sent the McIvers a telegram this morning notifying them to contact you. I didn't expect you so soon."

"They knew we were in Tishomingo at the Fisher Hotel, so they wired us there. I'm Frank Barnes and this is my partner, Lee Clark." Both men shook John's hand again and then sat down.

"Tell us what's going on," Frank said.

"I recently held a large dinner party here at the house. The day after, I had the outhouse cleaned out. The scavenger man found a gun buried in the pit. That same day my daughter saw a body floating in the creek. It turned out to be our friend, Bois d'Arc. When we pulled him out, he looked like he'd been dead for a while. We put him in the barn. I knew you would want to see him before we took him to his kin."

"You did the right thing, Mr. Prichett," Lee spoke up. "We'd like to see the body."

John led the men to the barn and brushed the straw off the top of the handmade casket. "It looks like he was shot in the head. For the life of me, I can't figure out why anybody would kill Bois d'Arc." John stepped back while the two men lifted the lid to inspect the body. A strong odor belched from the coffin. They quickly stepped back, grimaced, and turned their heads away.

"Phew, his body is pretty rank. He needs to get in the ground," John lifted his shirt to cover his nose.

"We're going to have to open his head and dig the bullet out," Frank said. "We need a chisel, a hammer, and a knife."

"Sure, I'll be right back." John returned shortly and handed the items to Frank.

For the next several minutes there was an unnatural silence in the barn, interrupted only by an occasional *thunk* caused by the sound of the hammer and chisel breaking Bois d'Arc's skull.

Out of curiosity John looked and saw Frank's fingers disappear inside the dead man's head. He quickly turned away, feeling queasy.

A few seconds later Frank said, "I found it." He held a cartridge between his fingers and thumb, inspecting it, and then held out his hand to show Lee and John. "Looks like a .38 caliber." Frank took his handkerchief and carefully wrapped the bullet in the cloth before putting it in his pocket.

Lee gathered the tools and set them aside. "You might want to wipe these off before putting them away."

"My hired help will take care of them," John said, handing Frank a rag to wipe his hands.

"The body needs to be cleaned up before giving him to his family," Frank commented.

"Yes, we'll do that. Come this way and I'll show you the pistol."

The men followed John to the water pump where he picked up the slop bucket and dumped the contents on the ground.

Frank bent over and picked up the gun. "Well, look what we have here," he said, examining it carefully. "This gun happens to be a Colt 1877. The bullet we just removed from your friend's head and the one that killed Francis Kirby look to be the same caliber as this revolver." John handed Frank his handkerchief. "Thanks," Frank said as he wiped off the gun. "We'll hold it for evidence." He slipped it into his pants pocket then asked, "John, is there anyone you can think of who might have done this?"

69

RETURN TO OKLA CHUKA

"Nope. I'm as puzzled as you are about these killings," John replied.

"Do you know when Amos Brooks was last in Tishomingo?" Frank asked.

"I doubt he gets over this way much. The last time I knew he was in town was when he moved Gentle Woman from the ranch to her house in Ardmore and that was a few years ago."

"If you think of anything that might be helpful to our investigation, you can reach us at the hotel," Frank said. He started to shake John's hand then stepped back and smiled. "Sorry, don't think you want to shake this hand until I can get washed up."

John glanced over at the clothesline and saw several rags hanging out to dry. "I'll get some soap and give you something to dry your hands on."

Just then Ples came across the pasture on his way back from the hog pen. "These men need some soap," John yelled.

"There's plenty in the barn. I'll get it for y'all." In a flash Ples was at the pump with a bar of soap in his hand.

"This is Ples, my overseer. He takes care of everything around here. I don't know what I would do without him," John said.

Ples grinned from ear to ear.

◇◇◇

Late that afternoon Osi and Koi returned to Okla Chuka. Obviously hearing them arrive, John walked out onto the porch and spoke to Osi before he had time to get out of the buggy. "The investigators were here this afternoon. They dug the bullet out of Bois 'd Arc's head. It was the same caliber as the one that killed Kirby, and they think maybe both bullets came out of that gun the scavenger man found."

Koi jumped from the buggy, ran up the steps, and waved at her father before disappearing into the house. Osi took a seat on the porch.

"The investigators are staying downtown at the hotel. They want us to let them know if we suspect anyone," John continued.

"I've been meaning to ask if you thought the Jacksons were acting strange the other night," Osi replied.

"I didn't notice anything out of the ordinary. They always act like they're hiding something. It's hard to believe that Jennie McIver is related to them," John said. "Oh, here," he added. He reached into his pocket and handed Osi an ochre-colored envelope. "A messenger from the telegraph office delivered it this afternoon."

"It's from Isaac Roberts, the Cherokee man I met on the train," Osi said as he took the envelope. "He's the man I told you about wanting to form a new state separate from Oklahoma Territory. He said they want to call the new state Sequoyah and it will only consist of the Nations of Indian Territory. We'll be out-voted if both territories are combined, so I'm in agreement with him. We need our own state." Osi tore open the envelope and read the message.

```
TO JORDAN OSI NANCE
CHICKASAW NATION
TISHOMINGO I T

SEQUOYAH CONVENTION MEETING STOP
AUGUST 28 EUFAULA STOP

FROM ISAAC ROBERTS
CHEROKEE NATION
TALAQUAH I T
```

"There's going to be a meeting at Eufaula in a couple months. Do you want to go with me?"

"I might," John said. "We'll see when the time comes." He looked toward the barn. "First thing in the morning, we need to get Bois d' Arc out of there and deliver him to his family before he putrefies. Rose and Stevetta cleaned him up this afternoon and did their best to make his head look normal."

Chapter Nine

Gentle Woman awoke before dawn and lit a fire inside the cast iron cooking stove. A few minutes later Rose stumbled into the kitchen, still half asleep. "Thought I heard something. What you doin' up so early, ma'am?"

"I figured I better get an early start. We need to prepare food so the men can take it to Lawa when they deliver Bois d'Arc's body. I couldn't sleep last night for thinking about her. It's gonna be hard without her husband. That family sticks to the old ways. They've got a bunch of children, but I don't know if they're much help."

"They be just fine, ma'am," Rose said. She reached for an apron and tied it on. "What you want me to make?"

"Let's cook up a batch of shuck cakes."

◊◊◊

Ples had the wagon and team ready when John and Osi got to the barn. The three men tugged and pulled the coffin from the stall, lifted it, and carried it to the wagon.

"We're gonna need some rope to tie this down," John said, and Ples rushed to the barn to find some.

"I think I'll ride Black Panther ahead and let Lawa know about Bois d'Arc before you arrive with the casket," Osi told John.

"That's a good idea," John replied.

Ples returned with a rope and secured the coffin to the wagon bed just as Gentle Woman and Rose came out the door, each carrying a large basket of food.

Osi reached for the one in Gentle Woman's arms. "Here,

let me take that."

"Thank you, but I am not helpless," she said.

"I know you aren't, but that looks heavy." Osi stowed Gentle Woman's basket in the wooden box beneath the wagon seat. He then took the one from Rose and squeezed it in. "There, those should be just fine."

With Kash on her hip, Koi walked outside to see the men off. "Y'all have a safe trip," she said, waving Kash's tiny hand up and down.

Osi strode over to Koi and gave her a quick peck on the lips then patted Kash on the head. "We'll see y'all around dark." He waved at Kash as he made his way to the barn.

John and Ples were waiting in the wagon when Osi came out on his horse. "Rose, don't bother with supper for us. We'll eat with Lawa before we come home," John said.

The women stood watching as Osi led the way out the gates of Okla Chuka.

◊◊◊

Lawa was standing in the yard when Osi rode up. "*Chokma*," she said when he got close enough to hear.

"*Chokma*," Osi replied.

She invited him inside and pointed to a mat on the dirt floor where he took a seat.

She didn't speak English so Osi began speaking Chickasaw. "Bois d'Arc was found dead in the creek. John's bringing him by wagon." He didn't mention that her husband had been shot. That would have to come later when she asked.

Lawa remained silent, just looking off into space. Several awkward moments passed before she let out a loud wail.

Osi's first thought was to comfort her, but he sat quietly, knowing it was protocol for the bereaved to mourn alone.

Bois d'Arc's ranch consisted of several small huts behind the main house. Like most Chickasaw families, they lived in close proximity to each other. Upon hearing Lawa's wails, several family members came running. Osi met them at the door to explain that Bois d'Arc was dead and why Lawa was crying.

73

Then he stepped outside to give the family time alone and to wait for John and Ples.

Osi wasn't sure if the grown men going in and out of the house were Bois d'Arc's boys or nephews, but it didn't matter. They all considered him their father. He didn't know the minute details of a burial ritual, but he knew enough to ask if they wanted the casket brought into the house when the wagon arrived.

One man said, "Bring him inside."

Men, women, and children made a large pile of wood in the yard. All the while Lawa continued to wail. She cried even louder when John and Ples pulled up in the wagon.

Several men went to unload the casket. They carried it inside the house and placed it in the center of the room. By now everyone had gathered in the house with the corpse, except for Osi, John, and Ples.

After an uncomfortable quiet moment, drums and terrapin shell rattles could be heard thumping the rhythm of a beating heart. Lawa's wails rose and fell like the ocean tide as she continued to mourn.

One woman came outside the house and ran to one of the distant huts. She soon returned, carrying a colorful handmade quilt. John knew traditional Chickasaws believed the deceased needed to keep warm.

Osi, John, and Ples stood by the wagon. They could hear Lawa's cry when the drums paused. It was over an hour before three men came out of the house. They went to the woodpile and lit some kindling. It started as a small spark and then exploded into an untamed ball of flames.

John wanted to go back to Okla Chuka, but he knew that would be rude, so they continued to wait by the wagon. People walked out of the house, carrying small bundles. They went to the burning pile and threw them in the flames.

"They are getting rid of his belongings," John said. "They'll put his prized possessions in the casket with him. The rest of his things will be burned.

"I've heard that's the way they used to do it," Osi said.

"Yes, it keeps his spirit from coming back into our world. The bumps and creaks you hear during the night are believed to be the spirits of the dead coming to look for their possessions. You want to make sure everything that belongs to the deceased is burned, unless you want to be haunted," John smiled. Osi was all ears. He wanted to know more about Chickasaw customs before they were gone forever.

Ever since missionaries had converted the Chickasaws to Christianity, the old ways faded with each generation. There were a few exceptions, like Bois d'Arc and his family, who continued to cling to the old traditions.

"I'm glad Rose and Stevetta put new clothes on Bois d'Arc's body. That's one less thing the family has to do," John said.

Osi shuffled his feet and looked toward the door. "I wonder if they've opened the casket yet? Surely someone will have something to say when they see his head."

◊◊◊

Inside the house women wailed, moaned, and shook their rattles while the men continued to drum.

"No one has said anything about eating," Osi said. "I suppose they're too busy mourning to want food, but I sure would like some nourishment. Do you suppose they won't eat today?"

"I don't know. Sometimes, the family won't eat until the body is in the ground. But we should be leaving. It'll be dark soon." John reached under the buggy seat and lifted out a basket of food. "Let's go talk to one of Bois d'Arc's sons before we take off."

Osi picked up the other basket and walked with John to the house. Cedar wood and sage smoke crept out the open door. The pungent smell caused John's and Osi's eyes to burn, and they coughed when they walked inside the crowded room. Two women took the baskets from them and went away without saying a word.

The casket lid was open and the colorful quilt had been placed over Bois d' Arc's body. His head and hands were the only parts left uncovered. On top of the quilt lay a few ears of

75

corn, several feathers, a bundle of sage, a twist of tobacco, a braid of sweet grass, and piece of red root. Near his right hand they had placed his hunting knife.

John and Osi stepped up to the casket to show their respect. The drums and wailing softened to a low tone. John spoke kind words in Chickasaw about his friend. He bent over, took a pinch of the red dirt from the floor, and dropped it in the casket. Osi didn't know the meaning of the gesture, but he followed suit.

John wondered if Lawa would insist they bury Bois d'Arc under the dirt floor in the house, as was the old custom, or take him to some hill on the property.

Lawa stopped wailing and came to stand next to John. "Where's Bois d'Arc's gun?" she asked in Chickasaw.

"He didn't have a gun on him when he was pulled from the creek," John said.

"Where are the clothes he was wearing?"

"I'll go get them for you." John walked to the wagon. "Ples, where's Bois d'Arc's old clothes? They need to burn them."

"Rose stuffed them here." Ples wrinkled his nose as he carefully pulled them out of the wagon. "They's awful nasty."

John took the garments from Ples, returned to the house and handed them to Lawa, who immediately started looking through the pockets. Not finding anything, she looked up at John. "He was never without his gun. He always carried it in his pocket." She became agitated, her eyes widened, and she screamed, "I need to put it in the coffin with him. He needs it. We can't bury him without it!"

"I'm so sorry, Lawa, but he didn't have a gun on him," John replied. Osi knew John was being evasive with his answer. "When did you last see Bois d'Arc?" John asked.

"The afternoon he left here to go eat at your house."

"Well, he never made it to the dinner party."

It was long after midnight when the men arrived back at Okla

Chuka. A single kerosene lamp burned in the parlor, with a faint golden glow that could be seen all the way to the gate.

"Looks like someone is waiting up for us," Osi said. "You go on in, John. I'll take care of Black Panther before I come in." He rode to the barn to feed, water, and groom his horse while Ples stopped the buggy at the house to let John out before going to the barn as well.

John walked into the house and waved goodnight to Koi when he saw her in the parlor. "Osi will be in soon," he told her. "But I'm tired, so I'm off to bed."

When Koi heard Osi coming in the back door, she put her book aside and went to him. "I couldn't sleep until you got home. With the killings lately, I was afraid something might have happened to you."

"We're fine. It was a long day with no food, but I'm too tired to eat right now. I'll tell you all about the trip tomorrow," Osi pulled her close and gave her a goodnight kiss.

◊◊◊

"Rose, your biscuits keep getting better all the time."

"Mista Prichett, Miz Gentle Woman made these this mornin'."

"Well, they taste mighty good, especially after not eating yesterday."

"Going without food for a day does make a person appreciate nourishment when it comes along," Osi said.

"It doesn't surprise me that Bois d'Arc's family didn't eat. They might not eat for a few days," John said.

Gentle Woman frowned. "I sure hope they do, 'cause if they don't, all the food we sent will be wasted."

John looked at her and smiled. "I'm sure it will get eaten. The children will probably sneak into the house and get it."

"Will they bury Bois d'Arc without his gun?" Osi asked.

"That depends on Lawa. She insisted they can't put him in the ground until she's placed it in the casket with him."

Koi put her fork aside and stopped feeding Kash for a moment. "What's that about a gun?"

77

"Lawa said Bois d'Arc always carried a gun in his pocket. He didn't have one on him when we brought him here. Who knows where it is, maybe at the bottom of Pennington Creek." Osi took a sip of coffee. "We're going to Tishomingo to talk to the investigators as soon as we finish breakfast."

John pushed his chair back from the table. "I have a few things to do before I can leave. I'll holler when I'm ready."

"Let's go on the porch and wait," Osi said to Koi.

Koi handed Kash to Rose and followed Osi to the swing. She took a seat and began moving gently to and fro. Osi slipped in beside her. "What happened yesterday," she asked.

"It was a learning experience for sure. They did a lot of drumming and terrapin rattlin', and Lawa did a lot of crying. The only time she stopped wailing was when she asked John about Bois d'Arc's gun. One thing that really surprised me was your father's knowledge of old rituals. He knows a lot more than he lets on."

"He probably stored them in the back of his mind when he married Mother." Koi grinned. "When I was sick with Kash, your mother taught me herbal medicine," she said proudly.

"We need to learn all we can. The old customs are dying out. By the time Kash gets our age, they'll all be forgotten. We can't let him grow up without knowing the ways of our ancestors," Osi said. Koi nodded in agreement.

"I'm ready," John yelled from the great room.

Osi stood, gave Koi a quick peck on the cheek, and turned to go to the barn. Koi waved goodbye when the men rode past the house on their way to Tishomingo.

◊◊◊

Osi and John rode along Capitol Street to the O. Fisher building. It was one of the first buildings in Tishomingo where general merchandise was sold. Mr. Fisher also rented out rooms upstairs, so people generally called it the Fisher Hotel. Mr. Fisher was standing in the doorway when Osi and John rode up.

"How are you doing, Mr. Fisher?" John asked.

"I can't complain. How are you, Mr. Prichett?"

"We're doing all right. We came to see two gentlemen you have staying here," John said, swinging down from his saddle. He stepped onto the shallow boardwalk and his spurs clanked as he went to shake hands with Mr. Fisher. "Are Frank Barnes and Lee Clark here?"

"No, they left about an hour ago and didn't say when they'd be back, but you can leave 'em a note and I'll make sure they get it."

"That sounds good to me." John followed Mr. Fisher inside the building. Osi remained in the saddle and waited until John returned and mounted his horse. "While we wait for the investigators, let's go back to Okla Chuka by way of Pennington Creek and take a look," Osi said. "We can go upstream as far as the Foley dam and see if there's been a scuffle along the creek bank."

"We might get lucky and find Bois d'Arc's gun," John said, "but I doubt it."

◊◊◊

When Osi and John came through the gates of Okla Chuka, they saw two livery horses tied to the hitching post in front of the house.

"Looks like Mr. Barnes and Mr. Clark beat us here," John said.

"I didn't think we'd been gone that long, but it's nice to know they received your message and came so quickly," Osi replied.

Gentle Woman and Koi had welcomed the men into the great room and Rose had served them lemonade.

"Hello. I'm glad to see you made it here so soon," John said, entering the room. The men stood and offered a friendly handshake to both John and Osi. "Please have a seat. Can I offer you a cigar?" John opened his silver humidor for the investigators to see the contents.

"No, thank you. Not now. This lemonade hits the spot," Lee Clark replied. "We're eager to hear what you have to say."

John paused when Rose came into the room with

lemonade for him and Osi. When she closed the door behind her, John began. "We took Bois d'Arc's body to his ranch yesterday. His wife, Lawa, is very disturbed. She can't bury his body without his gun. Traditional Chickasaws believe the deceased must have their weapons with them when they go to the Happy Hunting Grounds."

Osi added, "Lawa was more worried about getting the gun placed in the casket than how he died. She never did ask about the wound in his head."

"That seems a little strange to me," Lee Clark said.

"It may seem strange to outsiders, but remember, they're traditional and they don't think the same way. To her he was dead and nothing was going to bring him back, so it didn't matter how he died."

There was a quiet pause in the conversation before Osi asked, "Do you suppose the gun found in the outhouse could be Bois d'Arc's?"

"That presents an interesting thought," Lee said.

Chapter Ten

"I suppose we should ask Bois d'Arc's wife if it's his gun," Frank said.

John leaned forward. "You need to be prepared for her to take it if it is."

Frank pressed his lips together. "Well, near as we can tell, the bullets that killed Francis Kirby and Bois d'Arc were both .38s, so they could have come from the same firearm. And the gun that came out of your privy was a .38. No way to tell for sure if the bullets came from the same gun, of course."

"Interesting," John shrugged. "I can't imagine who would do this."

"We aim to find out," Frank Barnes said. "When we left Chicago, our assignment from the Commissioner of Indian Affairs was to investigate corruption with land apportionment. We had no idea we'd be walking into this kind of situation."

Osi stood to stretch his legs. "Are you going to Bois d'Arc's place to question Lawa?"

"Yes," Frank said. "But we'll need an interpreter. Can y'all go with us?"

John and Osi both nodded.

"It's getting kinda late. We might ought to wait until tomorrow," John said, snuffing out his cigar.

Frank glanced at his pocket watch. "I'd rather get to it right away."

Lee walked to the door. "I'll ready our horses."

Osi turned to John. "I'll get our horses and meet you out front." Osi nodded to Rose in the kitchen. "Tell Koi and Mother we're going to ride out to Bois d'Arc's place with the investigators." He looked hungrily at the platter of fried chicken on the side table. "I think we'll need to take some of that with us, since we won't be back for supper."

"I'll fix you right up, Mista Nance." Rose quickly wrapped several pieces in brown paper, cut a large hunk of cornbread from a pan on the stove, and placed it all in a cloth bag.

"Mista Nance, here's y'alls food," she said as she handed him the bundle. "This should hold y'all for a while."

Osi smiled, took the food, placed it in his saddlebag, and the four men rode out of the gates of Okla Chuka and turned north along Kemp Avenue.

A few miles outside of Tishomingo, they saw several men on horseback riding hell-bent toward them. Osi lifted his eyebrows as they got near. "That looks like Bois d'Arc's kin."

"Yep, I believe it is." John sucked in a deep breath. "They're in a hurry to get somewhere."

John, Osi, and the investigators came to a dead stop to await the riders coming toward them at a full gallop. They quickly found themselves surrounded by Bois d'Arc's boys. The agitated men slapped their leather leggings with their quirts to keep their beasts riled up. The horses pawed the ground, breathed heavily, and snorted foam from their nostrils.

"*Chokma*," John said.

No one replied.

One man pulled his horse close to John and stared at him without speaking.

"We are on our way to talk to Lawa." John raised his voice so he could be heard above the commotion.

The man grunted, turned his lather-soaked horse toward Bois d'Arc's ranch, and motioned for them to follow. Several men rushed ahead when the leader gave them a signal to go, while two men flanked both sides to act as escorts. They rode silently all the way to the ranch.

The woodpile in the front yard was still burning when they arrived, but it was not the raging fire it had been when Osi and John were there last. It now glowed with red-hot coals. Occasionally, someone came out of the house and threw a log onto the heap to keep it going. The radiant heat could be felt several feet away.

"That feels pretty good," Osi said, reining Black Panther

to a stop near the pile of embers.

"Yep, I think a Blue Norther might be moving in." John looked at the sky. "We need to make this visit quick and get back to Okla Chuka before the brunt of it gets here." As if in warning, a gust of cold wind whistled around them. The men reached for their coats tied behind their saddles.

Two of Bois d'Arc's men stood by the front door like sentries.

"*Chokma*," John said, walking past them.

Neither man said a word.

"*Chokma*," Osi said, following John's lead into the house with the investigators. Their eyes burned from the smoldering cedar and sage that filled the room.

Bois d'Arc's coffin was still in the middle of the floor. The strong pungent smell of smoke couldn't cover the stench of the man's rotting body. All four men quickly reached for their handkerchiefs and covered their noses and mouths.

Lawa sat nearby, softly whimpering. She looked up when the men entered and stood as they got near. She was pathetic. Her hair was unkempt and matted, her face puffy, and she appeared gaunt in her dirty calico dress.

John spoke to her in Chickasaw. "Lawa, I want you to meet Mr. Barnes and Mr. Clark. They are investigators from the Commissioner of Indian Affairs in Washington,"

She looked them over with a suspicious gaze. "I don't like them," she said in Chickasaw.

"You don't have to like them. They are only here to help you find Bois d'Arc's gun."

Lawa grunted and stared at John through tiny slits in her swollen eyes. "We can't bury him until we have his gun."

"That's what we came to talk to you about. We found a gun in my outhouse and we're wondering if it might be Bois d'Arc's."

Lawa's eyes widened. "Let me see it!"

John turned to Frank. "She wants to see the gun."

"Ask her what it looks like first," Lee said.

"What kind was it?"

Lawa hesitated for several awkward moments. "It was a Colt .38 caliber."

All eyes were on Frank as he reached into his trouser pocket and pulled out a package. He opened the cloth, exposing a clean, shiny revolver, and held it for Lawa to see.

Lawa's big almond-shaped eyes widened again. "That's it!" she yelled and reached for the gun. Without hesitation, she grabbed it and placed it in Bois d'Arc's blackened hand.

The family rushed in at the commotion. The men, who had been unfriendly earlier, grinned at the sight of the gun. Lawa closed the lid on the coffin after all the family members were satisfied the gun belonged to Bois d'Arc. Only then did she motioned for John, Osi, and the investigators to sit.

The drums and terrapin shells that had been silent when they arrived now erupted with song. Lawa ordered the women to bring food and drink to the guests, and the most inhospitable man in the bunch offered them tobacco. They accepted his gift and lit up. Trays of food were offered, but the smell of Bois d'Arc's body caused them to lose their appetites. They took only enough to be polite and pretended to eat so Lawa wouldn't be offended.

After the meal John politely thanked Lawa and stood to leave.

"Wait! I'd like to question her about the gun," Frank said.

"That's not a good idea right now," John said. "Let them get Bois d'Arc in the ground. We can come back in a few days."

Osi walked to the door and looked outside. "I hope we make it back to Okla Chuka before the full force of this storm gets here."

The temperature had dropped like a rock. The ferocious arctic wind roared around the cabins and whipped into the pile of embers, causing flames to jump from the coals with each strong gust.

"Let's get a move on." Osi urged the others to leave. "Besides, I don't want to stay here and smell this stench any longer." He went to Black Panther and in one fluid motion swung into the saddle. "Rose packed us some fried chicken, if y'all are hungry."

The others shook their heads. "Not now," John replied, speaking for them all.

The four men rode away from Bois d'Arc's ranch,

84

bundled in their oilcloth coats. They had not anticipated the sudden decrease in temperature and weren't prepared to ride all the way to Okla Chuka with the cold wind blowing.

Midway between Bois d'Arc's ranch and Tishomingo, it began to rain. The cold water swirled around them as the horses trudged southward. Another drop in temperature caused the rain to turn to snow.

"It's time we ride single file so we don't get separated," John advised.

Osi came up from the rear, took Lee's reins, and handed them to Frank. He then took Frank's reins and gave them to John. John passed his reins to Osi and they rode single file with Osi leading the way.

The Norther turned from a biting cold wind and rain into a blinding blizzard. In no time at all, a blanket of snow covered them. The party looked like ghosts slowly floating along the road.

Osi squinted, trying to see something familiar so he could get his bearings. In the distance he made out a faint light coming from the log cabin that stood in the middle of Kemp Avenue. He breathed a sigh of relief and yelled to the others. "We're almost home. Odell's place is just ahead."

The weary travelers pulled into the barn at Okla Chuka long after midnight. "You men are welcome to stay here tonight," John said to Frank and Lee.

"We're much obliged," Frank said. "I don't think I have ever been so cold in all my life. This weather is worse than anything we've ever experienced in Chicago."

Ples heard the men talking and came from his quarters.

"We're chilled to the bone," John told him.

"Y'all get inside. I'll mind the horses."

Osi grabbed the package of chicken and cornbread from his saddlebag. "Don't know about y'all, but I have worked up an appetite."

The men stomped the snowy slush off their boots and brushed the ice flakes from their coats before walking into the house.

"I sure could use some hot coffee," John said.

Osi lit the kerosene lamp and carried it through the house

to the great room where he sat the bundle of frozen food on the hearth. "Come in here. There's still a fire in the fireplace and it feels good."

Gentle Woman and Rose were awakened by the men's voices and came into the room.

"I am so glad to see y'all are home safe. We thought you might have decided to stay at Bois d'Arc's and not venture out into this weather," Gentle Woman said.

"We couldn't stay. You can smell Bois d'Arc's body a mile away," John exaggerated.

The other men cracked a smile.

"Mista Prichett, would you like for me to make something for y'all to eat?" Rose asked.

"We sure would like some hot coffee," John said. He pointed to the bundle Osi had placed on the hearth. "We can eat the food you packed for us, but we need to get out of these wet clothes first. Frank and Lee will be spending the night, so show them to a room and get 'em some dry clothes."

Osi went to his room to change and wasn't surprised when he was interrupted by a knock on his door. "Come in, Koi," he said, instinctively knowing it was her. When she slowly opened the door, he gazed at her in her nightgown, holding a lit candle.

"I am so glad you're home safely," she said.

Osi, half-dressed, pulled her to him. He quietly closed the door, blew out the candle, and set it on a table. He held her close and gently kissed her on the neck, working his way to her lips before nudging her toward the bed. He unbuttoned his wet trousers and let them slide to the floor. Folding back the heavy quilts, he crawled naked into the bed, pulling Koi under the covers with him.

The Blue Norther passed during the night. By morning, the clouds were gone and the sky was a brilliant azure blue. The only reminder of the previous night's storm was a biting chill in the air.

The sun's first rays crept through the window curtains, waking Osi. He rolled over and reached for Koi. She wasn't beside him. He lay back and rested his head on the goose-down pillow. His thoughts flashed from visions of Koi to his responsibilities at the ranch. He had not planned to stay away this long when he came to attend John's dinner party, but one thing after another had caused him to postpone leaving. After last night's storm, he was concerned about his livestock and wondered if the wranglers had been successful in getting them to shelter.

Osi quickly dressed, splashed cold water on his face from the washstand pitcher, and walked to the kitchen with his dirty, wet clothes in hand. "Good morning, ladies," he said to Rose and Stevetta, who were already preparing breakfast. "Here's my wet clothes from yesterday," he said, handing them to Stevetta. He watched Rose pour his coffee. "I'm ready for a cup of that java. It sure smells good." He carried his coffee to the great room and waited for the others to get up.

Soon everyone began gathering in the dining room for breakfast.

"Good morning," John said. "Looks like the storm cleared and it's gonna be a nice day today." He designated where he wanted Frank and Lee sit by waving his hand near the chairs. "Osi, what happened to you last night? You didn't come back to the great room after changing," John said.

"I was tired." Osi said and slyly smiled at Koi. "I'm leaving right after breakfast to check on things at the ranch, but I'll be back as soon as I make sure my wranglers have everything under control." He nodded at the investigators. "You won't be needin' me for a while, will you?" They shook their heads. "Good, then I'll be on my way after we eat."

Chapter Eleven

After breakfast the family stood on the porch and waved goodbye to Osi and the investigators as they rode out of the gates.

"Father, I have something I want to talk to you about."

"Of course, Koi, let's go into the great room."

Koi handed Kash to Gentle Woman, and they walked into the house. She took a seat next to her father's chair while he fumbled through the humidor for the cigar he wanted.

"What's on your mind?" He lit the cigar and sat down.

"Ever since we got back from Chicago, I've been thinking I would like to start a school of art and music for the children of Tishomingo."

"That's an admirable idea. Where do you think this school should be located?"

"I was hoping we could build one right here at Okla Chuka. We're not that far from town and a wagon could bring the children each day."

John smiled. "It sounds like you have the details worked out."

"Well, the idea has been floating around in my mind for a long time."

John grinned. "I don't see any reason why we can't do it. It's not like there isn't enough space."

Koi jumped up, threw her arms around her father, and gave him a big kiss on the cheek. "Thank you. You're the best father in the whole wide world."

"Let's go for a walk and see where this building would be most suited."

"I'll get my shawl and meet you on the porch."

John and Koi walked the grounds of Okla Chuka, looking for the best place for a schoolhouse. They were discussing the pros and cons of each location when a buggy came through the gates and pulled up to the house.

"Look who's here! It's Jennie and Matthew." Koi hurried to them. "I am so glad to see you."

Jennie handed baby Jacob to Koi before she stepped down from the buggy. "I'm happy to be here. I swear that trip from Ardmore gets longer all the time, especially holding a squirming child."

"*Chokma*," John greeted Matthew. They shook hands and together they took the buggy to the barn.

"Let's go inside so you can relax and Rose can fix us some tea," Koi said, walking onto the porch. She shifted the baby in her arms. "Goodness, Jacob's getting heavy." She opened the door with one hand. "Gentle Woman," she called, "Come see who's here."

Gentle Woman laid her crocheting aside. "Jennie, it's so good to see you." Her eyes widened with amazement "Look how much Jacob has grown in such a short time."

"Where's Kash?" Jennie asked. "I can't believe he's over a year old already."

"Rose put him down for a nap. He should be up soon," Gentle Woman said as she reached to take Jacob. "Let me have that little one while you girls catch up on the latest news."

Koi raised her forefinger, signaling for Jennie to wait while she summoned Rose to bring tea to the great room.

Gentle Woman shifted Jacob on her hip. "Will you be staying awhile?"

"We'd like to stay a few nights. Amos Brooks and his sons are bringing our household goods in their wagon." Jennie smiled. "They don't travel fast, so I don't expect to see them right away."

Koi and Jennie took seats in the great room. "Have you and Matthew found a house?" Koi asked.

"Yes. It's a cute little white cottage on Nashoba Avenue not too far from Main Street. Matthew's happy he'll be able to walk to work."

"Wonderful. Let's take the buggy and go see it after

89

you've rested." Koi paused. "You just missed Osi. He left for his ranch not long ago."

Jennie gave Koi a playful smile. "We saw him on the road. He said he'd hurry back as soon as he could. I'm sure Matthew wants to know more about the details of Bois d'Arc's death. I hope the investigators find out who's behind these killings."

"Yes. It's pretty scary knowing there's a killer in our midst." Koi wiggled in her seat and leaned forward, clasping her hands. "Father and I were just outside planning where we should build a classroom."

"A school?" Jennie asked.

"Yes. I'm going to teach art and music to the children of Tishomingo. It's about time we have some culture brought to the Territory."

"That's exciting!" Jennie said. "I can hardly wait for our boys to attend."

"By the time they're ready for school, I should have everything running smoothly," Koi prophesied.

"If you need help in the classroom, you know where to find me," Jennie grinned.

◊◊◊

John and Matthew entered the house, letting the back door slam. "Yep, Koi wants to be a teacher and educate the younger generation in fine arts," John said proudly. Matthew grunted his acknowledgment as they walked into the great room. John continued, "How soon will you be opening your law office?"

"Right after we get settled in our new home. I don't want to bite off more than I can chew at one time." Matthew stepped over to Jennie, gave her a peck on the cheek, and took a seat next to her.

John went to his favorite chair, picked up his humidor, and offered Matthew a cigar.

"Don't mind if I do." Matthew selected a fine Havana.

"I'm sure you've heard a gun was found in our outhouse the day after the dinner party," John said.

"Yes. Those two investigators, Barnes and Clark, mentioned something about it when they were in Ardmore last. I want to hear all the details."

Koi realized if she and Jennie were to have a private conversation, they needed to go somewhere else. Likely, her father and Matthew would be talking for hours about the *incidents*.

Koi stood. "Come on, I'll show you to the guest room where y'all will be staying. You probably want to freshen up a bit after that long ride." She led Jennie down the hall and opened the door to the brightly decorated guest quarters and watched Jennie's eyes scan the room.

"You even have a baby bed in here. Koi, you think of everything."

"We never know when we'll have company with a little one," Koi winked. "When you're ready, we can go to town and see your new house. I'm sure Gentle Woman and the help can manage the boys."

"Okay. I'll see you in a few minutes." Jennie stepped to the washstand.

Nance Ranch

Osi arrived at his ranch to find two wranglers bending over a young heifer lying in the cattle pen near the house. "You boys need some help?" he called, sliding out of his saddle.

"Yep. She's a young'un. I think this calf is too big for her," one of the wranglers replied.

Osi surveyed the situation. The young bovine strained hard with each contraction. "Let's get her up," he said, pulling her to her feet with the help of the wranglers. "She's weak. How long has she been in labor?"

"Don't know. She was fine earlier this morning, but when we got back from chores an hour ago, she was down."

Osi took off his shirt and threw it on the fence. "One of you men go and get a rope from the barn, and bring some lard from the kitchen." He tried to reach his hand inside the cow to determine the calf's position, but the vulva was dry. "Hurry up with that lard," he yelled.

"Here." The wrangler handed Osi a wooden tub of soft grease.

Osi grabbed a handful and slathered it on his right hand and arm, all the way to his shoulder. This time his hand slid in easily, and he gently forced his entire arm inside the birth canal. He stepped aside to keep from getting splashed when the cow's water broke. Osi took his time feeling for the calf's head. He had to make sure it was not hitting the pelvic bones. If he could get his hand between forehead and the lining of the uterus, he knew he could pull it out.

Breathing a sigh of relief when he determined the fetus was in the correct position, he withdrew his arm and turned to the wrangler holding the rope. "Hand me that," he said. He tied a slipknot onto one end then rubbed lard along the entire length. Holding the knotted end, he reached inside, feeling for the calf's front feet. Finding them, he wrapped the cord around its legs, withdrew his arm, and stood back. "You men come help me pull," he said.

The men stepped up behind Osi and took hold of the rope.

"Now, don't pull until she has a contraction. We'll need steady pressure, but let up when she stops pushing. This may take a while. We have to be patient." Both men nodded and watched the cow.

Soon the heifer began to push. All three men pulled on the rope, slow and steady. All at once another rush of liquid gushed out and tiny legs protruded, followed by the calf's body. Another contraction and suddenly the calf hit the ground. Osi bent down to check the newborn. "I've got to clear the nostrils," he said. He wiped away the slimy mucus with his hand and the calf began to breathe. "Looks like we got us a healthy one," Osi smiled. He walked away and leaned against a fence post, leaving the wranglers to finish up.

The men quickly untied the rope from around the newborn's legs and left the pen. Osi watched the new mother as she began licking and nurturing her baby. The miracle of birth never ceased to amaze him. He looked to the sky and gave a quick thank you to Ababinnili for another healthy calf then he went to the water trough and washed his hands and arms before retrieving his shirt from the fence. Exhausted, he went inside the house, realizing he had lots of hard work ahead of him at the ranch.

◊◊◊

Ples readied Gentle Woman's small buggy for Koi's and Jennie's ride into town. He brought it to the front of the house just as the women came onto the porch.

"Thank you, Ples." Koi stepped into the buggy and took the reins. Jennie lifted her dress, placed her foot on the step, and hoisted herself up.

When they arrived in town, Koi turned the buggy north from Main Street onto Nashoba Avenue. "You'll have to tell me which house."

Jennie pointed to a quaint little cottage that sat back from the street. A gravel drive went right up to the front porch. Koi stopped the buggy next to the hitching post and tied Bess to the railing. "Can we go inside?"

"Of course, it belongs to Matthew and me," Jennie said proudly. "It even has a porch swing like the one you have at Okla Chuka."

"I've spent many hours in our swing over the years," Koi reminisced.

Jennie talked a mile a minute, explaining where each piece of furniture would go and how she was going to decorate each room.

"Have you and Matthew decided what to name your place?"

"We're thinking of calling it "McIvers' Manor." Before Koi had time to comment, Jennie said, "Let's go out back and I'll show you the storm cellar."

"I doubt you'll need that for storms. An old Chickasaw legend says a cyclone will never hit Tishomingo because it sits in a hole and it's near the convergence of two rivers," Koi said.

"That's what I've been told, but I'm glad we have it, just in case. I like to be on the safe side, and besides, it's perfect for storing food." Jennie smiled. "I can't wait for the furniture to get here."

Okla Chuka

John and Matthew spent time in the great room, discussing politics and religion, smoking cigars, and trying to figure out who killed Bois d'Arc and Francis Kirby.

"The investigators wanted to question Lawa when they gave her Bois d'Arc's gun, but I didn't think it was a good idea at the time. Bois d'Arc's body wasn't in the ground yet." John blew a ring of smoke. "I'm thinking that I can get more information out of her if I go see her alone."

"I'm sure of that. She's liable to clam up with them there. I hope she can give you some clues as to who might have committed the crimes." Matthew flicked the burnt end of his cigar into the ashtray.

"Lawa said Bois d'Arc was on his way to Okla Chuka the night he was killed. The culprit had to be someone who was here. For the life of me, I can't imagine who it could be. Do you know of anyone at the party who might have cause to kill Bois d'Arc?" John asked.

"Wish I did, but no one I know of would have a reason," Matthew said.

The conversation moved from the shootings to Amos Brooks and his family's destitute situation.

"Has he been let off the hook for Francis Kirby's murder?" John asked.

"I believe so. The investigators were in Ardmore recently and told my father they were going to talk to the sheriff and get the charges dropped. Poor Amos, he seems to be going from bad to worse when it comes to making a living for his family. Raising cotton isn't profitable for him, and Francis Kirby is no longer around to give him bank loans. Jennie and Mother delivered food to Sally last week, but who knows how long that will last. Amos needs a job that will make him enough money to provide for his family."

John nodded. "I'll agree to that."

94

"I suggested he might consider going into the furniture-moving business. His sons are big enough now to help him, especially Fletcher. When I mentioned the idea to him, he seemed to like it. The biggest problem I see is that he lives too far away. He'll have to move if he wants to go into business."

"Are you thinking of Ardmore or Tishomingo?" John asked.

"Tishomingo. With the opera house and all the other new buildings going up, he could get plenty of work. If he moved here, would you be willing to help me get them situated?" Matthew asked.

"I suppose so. I know Gentle Woman and Koi are fond of Sally and have always done what they could to help them out."

"The first thing is find them a place to live. That won't be easy with all those children."

"I might be able to alleviate that problem," John replied. "I own a place east on Main Street. It's located at the top of the hill as you head out of town. The house is in pretty bad shape and will need some major repairs to make it livable, but I'm sure we can manage."

"My father and I will pitch in with funds to get it done," Matthew offered. "I'll ask Amos if he wants us to help him get a business started when he brings our furniture. I hope he doesn't linger long on the road, we're eager to get settled."

"Amos is never in a hurry to get anywhere as long as he has bay rum to drink," John said.

"If he moves to Tishomingo, maybe we can wean him off that stuff. He'll have to straighten up if he wants to be a successful businessman," Matthew said.

"That might be a problem. He has to be the one to want it. We can only help him to a point," John said.

Chapter Twelve

John and Matthew rode along Main Street looking at the new construction. "You picked the right time to open a law office," John said. "Tishomingo is booming."

As they hitched their horses to the railing in front of the bank, a courier from Western Union stepped up. "Mr. Prichett, sir," the young man said. "I have a telegram for Mr. Nance. Is he at your house?"

"No, he's at his ranch, but I can see that he gets it."

The delivery boy handed John the envelope. John reached into his pocket, pulled out a coin, and gave it to the boy. "I suppose I'll need to ride out to Osi's place in a few days and deliver this." He turned the envelope over in his hand. "Looks like it's from the men in Tahlequah, the ones trying to bring Indian Territory into the Union as a new state called Sequoyah." He stuffed the envelope into his vest pocket and turned to Matthew. "Let's go have a look at your new office."

Matthew opened the bank door before he saw a furniture-laden wagon slowly coming down Main Street. "We'll, I'll be, there's Amos!" He smiled and walked toward the wagon. "Come on, let's go meet him."

"I know what we'll be doing the rest of the afternoon." John laughed then followed his friend.

"How was your trip, Amos?" Matthew asked.

"It was all right. I didn't break an axle coming across those gullies and that's a good thing." Amos grinned.

"We'll walk alongside the wagon and show you to the house." They turned north on Nashoba Avenue and Matthew pointed to the white cottage with the gravel drive.

"I see Koi and Jennie are still there." John pointed to

Gentle Woman's buggy parked out front.

Matthew rushed ahead, bounded up the front steps, opened the door, and yelled. "Jennie, Amos is here with our furniture!"

The women came rushing when they heard Matthew's voice. He repeated his message. "The wagon has arrived with our things."

Jennie grabbed Koi's arm and smiled. "He wasn't that far behind us."

"You better decide where you want everything," Matthew said. "We'll be moving it in right away."

"Y'all will still be staying the night with us, won't you?" Koi asked.

"Yes," Matthew replied. "We won't be ready to settle in tonight."

Amos' wagon squeaked and groaned as the oxen pulled the heavy load in front of the house. Matthew assumed a take-charge mode. "John, there's no need for you to lift anything. Amos and I'll unload, with the help of the boys. Jennie and Koi can tell us where to put things."

"Well, then, I better get back to Okla Chuka and see about getting them some food."

"Would you mind bringing my horse from the office before you leave?" Matthew asked.

When Matthew saw John leading his horse up the drive, he went to meet him. "Thanks, John."

John nodded. "I'll be back shortly." He waved goodbye and rode at full gallop all the way home.

◊◊◊

Ples stepped out of a nearby stall when John entered the barn.

"I need you to take care of Fancy," John said. "Amos and his boys arrived with the McIvers' furniture this afternoon. I'm gonna ride back into town as soon as I can get some grub for them." He walked in the back door, letting it slam. "Rose! Stevetta!" They both came running. "I need you to fix some food for Amos and his boys. They'll be staying in Tish' tonight and probably tomorrow night too. They've got a lot of household goods to unload."

Gentle Woman pushed the perambulator down the hall with Kash and Jacob perched inside. "John, you knew what you were doing when you bought this baby buggy. These boys have been entertained all afternoon with Rose and me giving them rides."

John grinned, leaned over, and ruffled each boy's hair. "These are some fine-looking boys." He reached inside his vest pocket, took out Osi's telegram, and showed it to Gentle Woman. "This came for Osi. It's from those Tahlequah men. Let Rose and Stevetta know it's here." He placed it on the tray by the front door and ruffled the boys' hair again before going to the kitchen. "You got that food ready?" he called to Rose.

"Yes sir, Mr. Prichett. It's right here." Rose handed him a bundle of food.

John sniffed the package. "Smells good. I better get it to them before I'm tempted to have a taste. We'll be home for supper around dark."

McIvers' Manor

John arrived to find Amos' oxen unhitched from the wagon and chomping on clumps of grass in the lot next door. Everyone was moving furniture and unloading the many wooden boxes of household goods from the wagon. "Y'all hungry yet?" he asked, sliding off of Fancy and retrieving the food from his saddlebag. He knew the answer and didn't expect a reply.

"Rose fixed this for Amos and his boys," John told Matthew. "Our food will be waiting for us when we get home. Are you about ready to call it quits for the night?"

"Yes. We're pretty tired," Matthew admitted.

When John handed Amos the bundle of food, he took it, leaned over, and spit a big chew of tobacco near John's boot.

"Amos, it's not polite to spit your tobacco where someone can step in it," John reprimanded him.

"I'm sorry, Mr. Prichett," Amos looked down in shame.

John shook his head, knowing poor Amos didn't know

any better, as the man and his boys turned and walked to their wagon to eat. Staring at the wad of chewing tobacco, John looked at Matthew. "Think we can teach Amos some manners, or is he a lost cause?"

"We're gonna have to try or he'll never make it as a businessman," Matthew said. "One thing for sure, he'll have to show us that he wants to better himself. Otherwise, we'll be doing all this help for nothing."

Koi and Jennie buttoned up their immediate project before climbing in the buggy.

"Amos, y'all can sleep in the house and make pallets on the floor if you want," Matthew said.

"No, Mr. McIver. Me and my boys is used to sleepin' in the wagon. We like to be out in the open air."

"Suit yourself. We'll see you in the morning."

Okla Chuka

Daybreak at Okla Chuka began with a rooster, perched on the front porch railing, crowing. His *cockle doodle doo* echoed throughout the house. Soon the household became a whirlwind of energy. Rose and Stevetta prepared breakfast while Koi and Jennie gave instructions to Gentle Woman on how to take care of the boys while they were gone.

"Don't let Kash climb on the furniture. He might fall and hurt himself," Koi said.

"Jacob needs a nap at two this afternoon," Jennie added.

"We seemed to do just fine yesterday," Gentle Woman replied with a smile. She wasn't offended by their remarks—she knew the protective behavior of new mothers. She just listened quietly and nodded her head in agreement. She would listen to her own instincts on childrearing and knew they had nothing to worry about.

During breakfast, John spoke to Gentle Woman, Rose, and Stevetta. "I doubt Osi will show up today, but if he does, don't forget to tell him that he has a telegram sitting on the tray." John looked at Rose. "And we need some more food to take to Amos. He and his boys' bellies are bottomless pits." Everyone at the table smiled. "You better throw in some extra food for us," John added. "We probably won't be home until dark." Before leaving, he grabbed two cane fishing poles from the barn and threw them in the back of the buggy.

McIvers' Manor

By mid-afternoon all the furniture and household goods were unloaded and in their proper places. Koi and Jennie worked diligently. Jennie organized the kitchen while Koi made the beds with fresh linens.

"We'll be staying here in our own home tonight, won't we?" Jennie asked when Matthew walked into the house.

"Not tonight." He wiped his brow. "I think we need to stay one more night with the Prichetts. John and I have business to discuss with Amos, and we wouldn't have time to get Jacob and our things and be back before dark. We'll see y'all there later."

He walked outside and stood beside John and Amos. "We finished earlier than I thought. Jennie and I never could have done this by ourselves. We sure appreciate your help." He pulled several silver dollars from his pocket and handed them to Amos. Amos smiled and reached out to take the coins.

"Amos, John and I want to talk to you about a business venture."

Amos looked perplexed. "I don't know much about business and don't know what a venture is, but if it's gonna make me some money, I want to know 'bout it."

John took advantage of the moment. "I brought a couple cane poles and thought your boys might like to go fishing in the creek while we go to town, have a cup of coffee, and talk."

Amos' face lit up. He grinned from ear to ear hearing John say they were going to town to have coffee.

John went to the buggy and retrieved the fishing gear. "You boys come over here," he yelled.

Fletcher and Ludie came running. John handed a pole to each. "You're gonna have to dig worms for bait. I think there might be some in the garden area." He pointed to a likely spot.

"Be back here before dark," Amos ordered as the boys

took off.

"Amos, you can stay here another night," Matthew offered.

"I think we might just do that." Amos paused and then kicked at the pea gravel beneath his feet. Still looking at the ground, he said, "I'm gonna go to the drug store before we go have our talk."

Matthew and John looked at each other in disgust. They knew they were going to have a hard time breaking Amos of his addiction to bay rum. It wasn't all that good to drink, but with the Territory being dry, it was all Amos could get his hands on.

◊◊◊

Amos took the bottle from his overalls, popped the cork, turned his head away, and took a big swig before putting the stopper back in the glass container. Thinking he was putting something over on John and Matthew, he slyly slid it into his pants pocket. "I'm much obliged to you'uns," he said as the three men walked to a café across the street from the bank.

"We'd like to help you and your family, Amos, if we can," Matthew said.

Mrs. Hooser was standing in the doorway of her restaurant, waiting for customers, when the men approached.

John tipped his hat. "Good afternoon. We'd like some coffee." He pointed to the back of the room. "There's an empty table."

They had barely sat down when Mrs. Hooser was at the table, with a steaming pot of coffee. Amos lifted his cup, poured the contents in his saucer, and started blowing on it.

"What are you doing, Amos?" John asked.

"I gots to cool it down before I can drink it." He lifted the saucer to his lips and began to slurp the brown liquid. Matthew and John ignored his lack of manners.

"We know you're having a tough time providing for your family," Matthew said. "My father and I have discussed your situation and think you would be well suited to go into the furniture-hauling business. I mentioned to John our desire to give you a helping hand. He's also willing to do what he can. What do you think of the idea?"

"I can't leave the farm with all them kids," Amos protested. "And Sally won't move. I can't even get her to go to Ardmore, and besides, I don't know nothin' about a movin' business."

"Well, give it some thought. John has even offered to let you and the family live at his property here in Tishomingo."

"At Okla Chuka?"

John spoke up. "No, my town property is located at the top of the hill, east on Main Street. The house isn't much and will need a lot of work before it's livable, but it's plenty big enough for your family."

Matthew gestured toward the window. "Do you see all the construction going on in Tishomingo? I'm sure you could make a good living. There aren't any other moving companies here, so there wouldn't be any competition."

After a long pause Amos said, "I never thought about moving to Tishomingo." He leaned back in his chair. "If I take you up on the offer, how do I know people'll hire me?"

"You can't be sure of anything in this life, but being an attorney, I will have contacts and I can recommend you as a good mover. You'll have to assure me you won't let me down and promise to do your best to make a go of it."

"Think about it, Amos," John urged. "We'll be back in the morning with the buggy so we can take you to see my property before you go back to Ardmore." He stood to leave, pulled a few coins from his pocket, and left them on the table. "Let's go home, Matthew. I'm tired."

Chapter Thirteen

The next morning Matthew, Jennie, and Jacob waved goodbye as they left Okla Chuka for their new home.

"I'm so happy Jennie and Matthew moved to Tishomingo," Koi said as she handed Kash to Gentle Woman.

"I'm going to follow them to town and show Amos the house before he goes back to Ardmore." John ruffled Kash's hair. "You be a good boy for your mamaw," he said as he stepped off the porch.

Koi frowned and her hands went to her hips. "When do you think we can get a carpenter to come give us an estimate on the schoolhouse?"

"I'll be getting construction workers to renovate the Tish' house for Amos, so I'll ask them to come here and have a look."

Koi's eyes sparkled. She rose up on her tiptoes and planted a kiss on John's check. "Have I ever told you you're the best father in the whole wide world?"

John grinned and suppressed a throaty chuckle. "A couple of times." He turned and headed towards the barn. "I'll see y'all later."

◊◊◊

As John slid out of his saddle and tied Fancy to the hitching post, he saw Matthew and Amos standing near Amos' wagon. "Y'all ready to go have a look at the house?"

"Yep, we were waitin' on you," Matthew said.

The three men climbed into Matthew's buggy and rode east on Main Street and John directed Matthew to the top of the hill. "Turn right, then south along the gravel road. I've let this house sit empty for a long time. No telling what condition it's in."

The house indeed looked neglected. Post oak trees had taken over the yard, and it was impossible to drive all the way up to the house. Matthew pulled the buggy as close as he could and the men continued on foot.

"This place is gonna take a lot of fixin' up," Amos said.

"I told you it needs work, but I can get some carpenters to make it livable," John said.

Amos turned his back to Matthew and John, reached into his pocket, and pulled out his bottle of bay rum. He took a big swig, drained the container, and threw it in the bushes. He then took a plug of tobacco and stuffed it into his jaw. His voice was muffled by the wad in his mouth, making him talk strangely. "Umkay, let's go hav' a luk."

"How did you like it?" Matthew asked Amos as they rode back to Tishomingo.

Amos leaned over the edge of the buggy and spit tobacco juice on the ground. "I been a-thinkin', he said. "It's a whole lot bigger than our place. And Sally might like that big cook stove in the kitchen."

"When you make a decision, let me know. Until then, I won't do anything about fixin' it up," John said.

Amos' team of oxen slowly pulled the wagon away from McIvers' Manor.

"I bet he stops at the drug store to get an ample supply of bay rum before he leaves town," John said.

"I hope he saves enough money to buy food for the family when he gets back," Matthew replied.

"There's not much I can do about fixing the house until Amos lets me know if he wants to move." John untied Fancy from the hitching post.

"Would you like to come in the house? Jennie can fix us

some coffee or lemonade," Matthew asked.

"Thanks for the offer, but I'll be on my way. I'm going to stop by Mark Odell's place and see if he's available to give me an estimate for building Koi's schoolhouse."

"She must really be serious about having a school at Okla Chuka."

"About as serious as one can get," John said. "I'll be on my way."

"Thank you for putting up with us these past few days."

John tipped his hat and turned Fancy in the direction of Kemp Avenue.

Okla Chuka

"Yoo hoo," John said, entering through the kitchen. Reaching the great room, he plopped down in his favorite chair, leaned toward the smoking table, and opened the humidor. He selected a cigar, snipped the end, and lit up.

"Father, are you home?" Koi yelled from the parlor when she smelled the cigar smoke.

"Yes, it's been a long day," he loudly replied.

By now Koi was standing in the doorway of the great room. "Did you talk to anyone about the schoolhouse?"

"Yes. One of the carpenters who worked on the capitol building is going to come by in a few days and see what you have in mind."

"I can hardly wait to tell Gentle Woman," Koi grinned.

Bois d'Arc's Ranch

The next morning John went to Bois d'Arc's ranch to talk to Lawa. He found her standing outside her house when he arrived. "*Chokma*," John said before dismounting.

"*Chokma*," Lawa replied.

"Lawa, I brought you a couple of chickens," he said in Chickasaw. He untied them from his saddle while she watched. When he handed them to her by their feet, she carefully looked them over, smiled, and motioned for John to come into the

105

house. Before stepping inside, a woman from one of the cabins came and took the chickens away.

Lawa pointed to a blanket spread on the red dirt floor. She sat down and motioned for John to have a seat. He plopped himself beside her and shuffled around, trying to get comfortable. "I came to see how you and the family are doing."

"Not too good," Lawa said.

"I was afraid of that. Is there something I can do to help?" John asked.

"You can catch the man that killed my Bois d'Arc."

"Do you have any idea who did it?" John asked.

"It had to be one of those Syndicate men."

"Why do you say that?"

"Because Bois d'Arc got rid of the one named Kirby."

John's eyes widened, trying to absorb what he had just heard. "Are you telling me that Bois d'Arc killed Francis Kirby?"

Lawa nodded her head.

"Why?" John asked.

"Kirby cheated one of our boys out of land that was due him. Bois d'Arc wanted to rid the Territory of those thieves."

"Do you know who these Syndicate men are?" John asked.

"No."

John realized he would get no more information from her, so he changed the subject. "Where did you bury Bois d'Arc?

Lawa stood and motioned for him to follow. They walked to a small hill a short way from the house. On top was a large mound of rocks. John was pleased to see a small white cross standing in the middle of the pile.

Lawa began to pray aloud while John stood silently at her side. He reached into his pocket, fumbling for something to leave on the grave. The only thing he had on him were a few coins and his pocketknife. He didn't really want to part with his knife, but it was the most appropriate gift he could leave, so he placed it between two rocks and walked away.

All the way home John thought about Bois d'Arc, Francis Kirby, and the Syndicate. This was a new turn of events, one he hadn't expected. He was eager to get home and contact the investigators.

◊◊◊

Gentle Woman sat her knitting aside when John arrived home. "I wondered if I was gonna have to send Ples to go look for you," she grinned. "How was your trip?"

"Very interesting! Lawa said Bois d'Arc killed Kirby."

Gentle Woman gasped. "I never figured Bois d'Arc would do such a thing."

"Lawa said Kirby cheated their son and Bois d'Arc wasn't going to stand for it," John said. "I'll be going to Tish' first thing in the morning to send a telegram to the investigators."

True to his word, after breakfast the next morning, John rode to Tishomingo. He went directly to the Western Union office and sent a message to the investigators in Ardmore, letting them know he had important news. He then walked to Harris' General Merchandise store to buy a pocketknife.

◊◊◊

It was two days later at breakfast when John thought of Osi's telegram. "No telling when Osi will get back to Tishomingo. I ought to ride out to the ranch and deliver it. It might contain a time-sensitive message for him."

Koi's face lit up at the sound of Osi's name. "Can I go with you?"

"I wasn't thinking of taking the buggy this time. I was going to ride Fancy."

"We don't need to take the buggy. I can ride Cricket," Koi assured him.

"All right." John winked at her. "Go tell Ples to get the horses ready and then pack an overnight bag. Let's get going right away."

Beaming with excitement, Koi rushed to get ready. She stuffed a change of clothes into her satchel and prepared a bedroll. With her belongings slung over her back, she turned and gave Gentle Woman and Kash a hug. "See you both tomorrow." She was glad she was no longer breast-feeding; it gave her a lot more freedom to pursue her own interests.

107

◇◇◇

John and Koi arrived at Osi's ranch only to find the cook alone at the house, preparing the evening meal.

"Good afternoon, Mr. Prichett, Miz Cooper," he said as they came in the door.

"Hello," John said. "Where's Osi?"

"He's down at the south pasture, fixin' the fence. I don't expect him back until dark."

"We're going to make ourselves at home. That trip from Tishomingo gets longer all the time." John smiled. "Whatever you're making sure smells good."

"It's Choctaw stew and hoe cakes, one of Mr. Nance's favorites."

◇◇◇

With time on her hands before Osi came back, Koi wandered through the house. She went to Gentle Woman's old room and opened the door. It was empty. She stared at the cobwebs hanging from the ceiling and then her eyes drifted to the dust-laden plank floor. Her thoughts were drawn back to the day she helped Gentle Woman move to Marietta Place. A little over two years was not that long ago, but thinking back, it seemed like a lifetime. Koi shook off the sentimental feeling and began to clean the room before bringing in her satchel and bedroll.

◇◇◇

Shortly before sundown, Koi heard Osi and the wranglers riding up. She looked out the window to watch them dismount.

"Looks like we've got company," she heard Osi say.

Koi saw his cotton shirt was damp with sweat and open to the waist, baring his bronze, hairless chest. As she watched, he slid out of the saddle in one fluid movement, causing her heart to skip a beat.

"You boys clean up and come to supper," Osi said to the wranglers before pushing the door open.

Koi waited by the window, her heart beating quickly.

"John? Koi?" Osi called.

"I'm in the parlor," John called.

"Where's Koi?" Osi started down the hallway.

Koi quietly snuck up behind him and grabbed him around the waist. "I'm here," she said.

He spun around and grabbed her in a bear hug before sitting her down. "Sure is good to see you."

"I came with a purpose," John said, stepping out of the parlor. He pulled the telegram from his vest pocket and handed it to Osi. "It came for you the other day, and I figured I better get it to you in case it contained something urgent."

Osi tore open the envelope. He took his time reading while John and Koi stood waiting. "Those men in Tahlequah have decided to postpone their August meeting until after the New Year," he said. "They don't have enough men to participate."

"I was afraid they'd have trouble getting representatives of each tribe together," John remarked.

Osi set the telegram on a side table, buttoned his shirt, and took Koi by the hand, escorting her to a chair. Before she could sit, he quickly plopped down and pulled her onto his lap. She chuckled at his playful antics and immediately stood, brushing her skirt to make sure it wasn't hiked up.

"You two act like a couple of kids." John smiled and shook his head.

"How long are y'all going to be here?" Osi asked.

"We'll head back to Okla Chuka in the morning. I notified the inspectors about news concerning Bois d'Arc, and they should be dropping by in the next day or two."

"What news?" Osi asked.

"Bois d'Arc killed Francis Kirby. Lawa said he cheated one of their sons out of some land. I never figured Bois d'Arc would have it in him to kill anybody."

Osi jerked his head back. "Me, neither. He must have been really angry to seek blood vengeance."

◊◊◊

The cook leaned out the back door and tapped the metal triangle with a large spoon, calling the wranglers to supper. A large slab of wood, placed along one wall in the kitchen, was being used as a table.

The men filed into the kitchen one by one. From the parlor Koi couldn't help noticing they strained their eyes to get a glimpse of her. She heard one say, "She be one of the most beautiful women in the Territory." Koi felt her cheeks grow warm.

Osi stepped into the kitchen as the men gathered at the table. The cook served each man a bowl of piping hot stew and placed a plate of hoe cakes between them.

"We'll be eating in the parlor," Osi told the cook. "I'll see you men bright and early in the morning. We need to practice our roping. There's gonna be a wild west show in Ardmore soon. We need to show those cowboys how to rope a calf." He smiled and walked back to the parlor.

◇◇◇

After supper John snuffed out his cigar. "I think I'll hit the hay early. It's been a long day."

Koi stood and kissed her father on the forehead. "Good night, sleep tight, and don't let the bed bugs bite," she said in a playful mood.

John smiled, shook his head, and went off to bed.

◇◇◇

Koi and Osi sat silently in the parlor. They could hear the cook rooting around in the kitchen, clanking pots and preparing food for the next day's meals.

"I need to get cleaned up after sweating all day. I probably smell like a cow," Osi said.

"I hadn't noticed," Koi politely fibbed.

Osi walked outside to wash at the hand pump while Koi went to Gentle Woman's old room. The setting sun gilded the treetops and shot the last beams of light through the window, giving everything in the room a golden glow.

She sat and removed her high-buttoned riding boots, wiggling her toes in delight at the freedom of being unencumbered. She removed her bodice, untied her skirt and under-garments, and let them drop to the floor before walking to the window. She moved the lace curtain and saw Osi drenching himself. She shivered at the thought of bathing in such frigid water.

From the corner of his eye, Osi caught a glimpse of Koi's golden skin when she let go of the curtain and walked into the shadows.

It was a warm night and Koi lay on top of the pallet with nothing covering her body. When she heard Osi come into the house, she turned on her side and pretended to be asleep. He stealthily crept into the room, unhooked his belt, and let his pants fall to the floor. He scooted them away with his foot and knelt on the padded blanket next to her.

A cool breeze came from the window, ruffling the curtains. The sudden change in air temperature blowing across her body caused her to move slightly.

"Stop trying to fool me. You aren't asleep," Osi said. He leaned over to kiss her. His cheek brushed against her silken hair that smelled of honeysuckle. An impulse of exciting energy shot all the way to his groin.

Koi pulled him to her. Osi's work-callused hands gently stroked her soft breasts. She sighed and then gasped when his lips moved over one of her nipples. He tickled it with his tongue. "Osi, stop that," Koi whispered. "You're going to make me laugh and wake up Father."

He didn't say a word as he continued to ravish her body.

After several minutes of delicious attention, Koi motioned for him to turn over on his back. She threw one leg over his abdomen and straddled him. Leaning forward, she wedged his head between her breasts. Pulling back, she touched his lips with hers. At that moment, excitement was so strong it rushed through them like a raging fire.

Osi was now at the portal of her womanhood. "I will love you forever," he whispered in her ear.

111

Chapter Fourteen

Early the next morning, Koi and John left the ranch and headed back to Okla Chuka. Koi blew Osi a kiss and waved goodbye as they rode away.

"Father, did Osi say when he would be coming to Tishomingo?"

"No, but I'm sure he'll be back as soon as he can take care of his responsibilities."

"I wish he'd move to Okla Chuka and give up ranching."

"Koi, there's no way he'd ever give it up, it's in his blood."

Koi remained silent as her father's words sunk in. She knew it was just wishful thinking on her part. Her thoughts shifted to building her school, and they rode without conversation the rest of the way home.

◊◊◊

Gentle Woman was sitting on the porch swing with Kash when John and Koi rode up.

"Yoo hoo!" Koi yelled from the gates. Gentle Woman carried Kash to the edge of the porch. "There's your mama." She encouraged him to wave.

Koi reined Cricket next to the porch and slid out of the saddle. She reached for Kash and gave him a hug and kiss. "How's my big boy?"

"Toss me Cricket's reins and I'll take the horses to the barn," John said.

Koi handed Kash back to Gentle Woman and stepped off the porch. She threw John the horse's reins, grabbed her satchel from the saddle, and scurried up the steps.

Gentle Woman let Kash slide out of her arms to stand on the porch while she opened the front door. He immediately ran for the steps. "Oh, no, you don't," Gentle Woman shouted. She grabbed him by his shirt collar and directed him inside the house. "That boy is getting to be a handful," she laughed. She sat him on the floor and dumped a box of toys next to him. "That should keep him occupied for a while." Brushing the dust off her apron, she turned to Koi, "How's Osi?"

"He's as fit as a fiddle and never looked better." Koi smiled. "He and the wranglers are getting ready for a wild west show coming soon to Ardmore. I was hoping he would come back to Okla Chuka with us, but it looks like he has too much work."

Gentle Woman walked to the foyer and took an envelope from the tray. "Koi, this letter came for you yesterday. It's from Claire Dubois, that woman in Chicago.

Koi reached for the letter and tore open the seal.

Dear Koi,

I hope this letter finds you and the family well. Eli and I have finally set a date for our wedding. We will get married June 10th of next year. It is hard to believe 1900 is just a few months away. I sure hope you and Osi can come to Chicago for the wedding.

I mentioned to Eli that I would like to visit you in the Territory. He suggested I take his train car and make the trip right away. He will be in Washington, D.C., doing his "senator business" for a few weeks. Are you up to having company?

Sincerely,
Claire Dubois
51 East Monroe Street
Chicago, Illinois

Koi's eyes widened as she looked to Gentle Woman. "We're fixin' to have company!"

113

◊◊◊

Koi waited until the next day to write a reply. She sat on the swing, trying to figure out how to start her letter. The rose-scented stationery box reminded her of Chicago. She remembered purchasing it in the hotel gift shop the day she met Claire. It seemed so long ago, and yet it had not even been a year. Her mind shifted back to the task at hand. She carried her box to the secretary desk in her room, took out a sheet of paper, and began to write.

> *Dear Claire,*
>
> *Congratulations! Thank you for inviting Osi and me to your wedding. I would love to attend. I'm not sure if Osi ever wants to set foot in Chicago again, but I'lll ask him.*
>
> *I''m looking forward to your visit. You won't find the Territory nearly as exciting as Chicago. Well, maybe it is as exciting, but not in the same way.*
>
> *We arrived home to find the Ardmore banker had been shot and killed. Those two investigators we saw at the trial came to the Nation to see if they could find the syndicate involved in Neville's scheme to rob us of our land. They're still in the Territory investigating. They visit our house every now and then to see if my father has any news.*
>
> *Do you remember Michael McIver, the lawyer from Ardmore? He announced at the celebratory dinner that his son, Matthew, and wife, Jennie, had a baby boy while we were in Chicago. Their baby, Jacob, is so cute. He is a few months younger than Kash, but Jennie and I have already planned for them to attend school together.*

114

Speaking of schools, my dream of building an Academy of Art and Music for the children of the Territory is about to become a reality. My father has agreed to have a schoolhouse built here at Okla Chuka. The carpenters are coming any day now to lay out the plans. I am so excited!

Osi is spending time at his ranch. We haven't married in a church ceremony yet. We're waiting until Neville has been gone a year. Father and I went to see Osi a few days ago. He and his wranglers are preparing for a wild west show soon. If you arrive in time, we'll go. You might find it a fun experience. Osi is the best calf roper in the Territory!

I look forward to hearing all about the society parties you and the senator attend.

Please bring newspaper advertisements showing the latest fashions displayed in Marshall Field and Company's windows. By the time we see pictures of the clothes here in the Territory, they've already gone out of style.

I can hardly wait for you to get here. Send me a telegram and let me know when you will be arriving in Ardmore so I can be there to meet the train.

Cordially,
Koi Cooper

Koi folded the letter and slid it into an envelope addressed to Claire. She looked in her reticule to see if she had money in it before hanging it on her wrist. Carrying the letter and her purse, she walked into the parlor. "I'm going to ride to the post office and mail this letter to Claire," she told Gentle Woman. "I won't be long."

When Koi arrived home, she saw her father in the yard,

talking to two men. She pulled Cricket up next to them and slid out of the saddle. "Hello," she said. Both men nodded.

"I'd like you to meet my daughter, Koi Cooper." John smiled. "She's going to be the teacher here, and she'll have the final word on how she wants her school built."

One man stepped up, "Pleasure to meet you, ma'am. My name is Mark Odell, and I'll be in charge of building your school. This is my son Arthur." The young man nervously shuffled his feet.

"Let's go inside and discuss what Koi has in mind." John directed the men toward the house.

Ples came from the barn and took Cricket. "Thanks, Ples," Koi said as she followed the men into the house.

John walked into the great room and picked up the humidor. "Would you care for a cigar?" he offered. "Please, have a seat and let's get down to business."

They spent the afternoon discussing the construction. It was near suppertime when the men stood to leave.

"We'll be back tomorrow to finish the plans." Mark said. "Then we can order the materials."

◊◊◊

The carpenters returned the next morning, finished their lumber list, and sealed the verbal contract with a handshake.

"I forgot to mention a bell. We need to have a big one, loud enough for the children to hear all the way to Tishomingo," Koi said.

"I'll see what I can do," John grinned on his way to the great room to smoke.

Koi found Gentle Woman and Kash in the parlor. "I think I'll give you a break from tending Kash today," Koi said. "I'm going to visit Jennie. I'll take him with me." She carried her son to her bedroom to get ready for the trip.

A half hour later, Koi lifted Kash into the saddle and then slid in behind him. He grabbed the pommel and held on tightly. "We're going to visit Jennie and Jacob today," she told him.

Koi knew he wouldn't reply and he probably had no idea

what she was saying, but she always talked to him like he was her equal. Gentle Woman stood on the porch and waved goodbye as they left the yard.

When they arrived at Jennie's house a little before noon, Jennie saw them coming up the long drive and rushed out to greet them. "Koi! This is a nice surprise! What brings you and Kash to Tishomingo?"

"I decided it was about time I pay you a visit so we can get caught up on the latest gossip." Koi smiled and tied Cricket to the hitching post, took Kash's knapsack from the back of the saddle, and carried the child and bag to the porch.

Jennie took the bundle from Koi. "I'll have Etta watch the boys while we have some tea."

"And who is Etta?"

"My help."

"You have help now?" Koi asked.

"Yes, I can't seem to manage Jacob with everything else that needs to be done around here." Jennie smiled then raised her voice. "Etta? We have company."

A neatly clad, uniformed maid came scurrying from one of the bedrooms. "Yes, Miz McIver?"

"My friend, Mrs. Cooper and her son, Kash, are here to visit."

Jennie handed Etta the knapsack. "Please take Kash to Jacob's room and entertain the boys while we talk."

Etta reached for Kash's hand. He grabbed her fingers and she led him down the hall.

"I can't believe he's not fussing." Koi shook her head in disbelief. "He's never gone with a stranger before."

"Jacob loves Etta. She has a special way with kids," Jennie said. "Come with me to the kitchen while I make us some tea. Would you like something to eat?"

"We ate before we came to town, so we're fine for now. If Kash gets hungry or thirsty, Etta will know. He fusses up a storm when he's hungry."

Jennie heated water in the tea kettle while she prepared the tea tray. When the kettle began to whistle, she poured the hot water into the china pot to steep, picked up the silver tray, and said, "Let's go to the parlor and visit." She poured two cups

117

before she sat down. "Now, let's hear the news."

Koi swirled the hot water in her teacup while she spoke. "I went to see Osi at his ranch a few days ago. He's preparing for a wild west show they're going to hold soon in Ardmore."

"We know who'll win all the prizes for calf roping," Jennie smiled.

"That's not all ..." Koi hesitated.

"What?" Jennie leaned forward and asked.

"Claire is coming to the Territory for a visit!" Koi blurted.

"Claire? Neville's girlfriend?"

"Yes. I told you she saved Osi's life by speaking up and telling what really happened to Neville. The least I can do is show my appreciation by entertaining her while she visits the Nation. I hope you'll accept her friendship as I have. Who knows, you might find you like her."

Jennie shrugged her shoulders. "We'll see," she said then changed the subject." Matthew received a telegram yesterday saying that Amos Brooks is going to take up the offer to move to Tishomingo."

"Did Matthew say when they would be arriving?" Koi asked.

"No, but you know Amos. It could be anytime."

"Well, that's liable to put a kink in my plans for a while."

"How does Amos and his family moving to Tish' have anything to do with you?"

"I was just getting ready to tell you that the carpenters came to Okla Chuka. They're in the process of ordering the lumber and will start building the school as soon as it arrives. But Father promised they'd work on the house for Amos. I hope they can get that old house fixed up for Amos and Sally before the lumber arrives."

"I'm so excited for you. I know how you've wanted the school. Do you have a copy of the plans so I can see what it's going to be like?"

"I don't have them with me, but if you come to Okla Chuka, I'll show you the spot we've chosen to build it. I told Father that we need a big bell, one big enough that it can be heard all the way to Tishomingo." Koi smiled.

"I'm looking forward to the day when our boys go to

118

school and become best friends like you and me," Jennie said.

"That time will come all too soon"

Jennie paused then grimaced. "I'm really concerned about my father."

"What's the matter with George?" Koi asked.

"Matthew and I had a visit from Luther the other night. As you know, my brother and Matthew don't see eye to eye when it comes to politics. I knew it must be something important or he wouldn't have come to the house."

"Is your father ill?" Koi asked.

"No, he's not sick. But Luther says he's been acting strange. He hasn't been himself since the dinner party at Okla Chuka. About a month ago two strange men came to see him. My brother said he had no idea what they discussed with Father, since he wasn't privy to their conversation. Then last week the marshal came to the ranch. Luther is concerned that our father might have gotten himself in some kind of trouble. He wants Matthew to represent him if he needs an attorney."

Koi sat quietly for a few minutes. "Those investigators from Chicago are here in the Territory, trying to find the men involved in the nefarious scheme to steal our Indian land," she said thoughtfully. "They know Francis Kirby and Neville were part of the Syndicate, and they're trying to find the others. Maybe they were questioning your father to see if he knows who might be involved. Surely George is innocent of any wrongdoing."

"You know I haven't been close to my family since I married Matthew, so I don't know what to think. These opposing political factions among our tribe rip families apart." Jennie teared up.

Koi stood and put her arm around her. "Don't worry until there's something to worry about. I'll always be here for you. Remember, we're blood sisters. Cross our hearts and hope to die."

Jennie cracked a little smile.

Chapter Fifteen

Okla Chuka

Koi slid out of the saddle and reached for Kash, who was hanging onto the pommel as if his life depended on it. "Kash, let go." Koi tried to pry his hands loose. Finally, he released his grip and she lifted him from the saddle. When he began to cry, she soothed, "I'll take you for a ride tomorrow. It's almost time for supper and we need to go indoors."

Ples came to take Cricket to the barn while Koi opened the door to the house and put Kash down. He took off running as fast as his little legs could carry him toward the great room, with Koi close behind.

"Papaw!" Kash said when he saw his grandfather sitting in his favorite chair.

John stood and scooped him up into his arms. "How's my boy?"

"He takes after you, Father," Koi said. "He'd rather be on a horse than eat."

John smiled.

"I thought I heard y'all talking," Gentle Woman said as she walked in and held out her arms. "Do you want to come to Mamaw?"

Kash leaned over for her to take him.

"I bet you're ready to eat after that ride." Gentle Woman turned and walked toward the kitchen with the little boy in her arms.

John sat and motioned for Koi to sit beside him. "What's new with the McIvers?"

"Quite a bit, actually. Jennie said Amos Brooks and his

family have decided to accept your offer. They'll be arriving any day to take up residence in the old house."

John lit his cigar and took a puff. "That means I better get the carpenters out there to fix the roof and put some doors on the place before they get here."

"I hope the work can be done before our lumber arrives for the school. Did the carpenters say when they could start framing?" Koi asked.

"No, but it'll probably be awhile before the supplies get here. Maybe someday the railroad will build a track through town. It sure would speed things up."

"Jennie's worried about her father. She said Luther came to see Matthew recently. He has a suspicion that George might be in some kind of trouble. The marshal and two strange men have been to the ranch to question him. She also said Luther wants Matthew to represent him if he's charged with a crime. It must be serious, because she broke down and cried."

"George and I've never seen eye to eye with our politics, but I've never known him to commit a serious crime. Speaking of crimes, though, I'm hoping the investigators will be paying us a visit soon so I can tell them what Lawa said about Bois d' Arc killing Kirby."

◊◊◊

A few days after John and Koi's conversation, John rode to Tishomingo to see how the carpenters were progressing on the house for Amos Brooks. When he arrived he saw the roof had been patched and new doors installed. A walking path from the gravel drive to the door had been cleared of weeds, brush and post oak trees.

"Yoo hoo!" John shouted as he approached the house.

Mark waved and climbed down the ladder from the roof to greet him. "Hello, Mr. Prichett. Glad you dropped by. Look around and tell me if there's anything else you want us to do."

"From what I can see, it looks pretty good."

"We only have a few things left to do. We should be finished by this afternoon."

121

"All right, come to Okla Chuka tomorrow and I'll pay you. When do you expect the schoolhouse lumber to arrive?"

"It'll probably be another week or so before it gets here."

John turned to leave. "Koi is looking forward to you starting on her schoolhouse."

"Once the lumber gets here, it shouldn't take us long," Mark said.

John swung into the saddle and rode Fancy to Matthew's office. He tied his horse to the hitching post and climbed the stairs to the second floor. When he opened the door and stepped inside the waiting room, a smartly dressed woman sitting behind a desk greeted him.

"Hello, sir. May I help you?"

"Yes, I'd like to see Matthew McIver."

"May I give him your name?"

"John Prichett."

"Just one moment." The woman stood and went to give Matthew the message. She returned in only a minute and held open the inner office door.

"Come on in here, John," Matthew called. "What brings you to town today?"

"I rode out to the old house to see how it was coming along. The carpenters will be finished today. You can let your father know that Amos and his family can move in anytime."

"I'll be making a trip to Ardmore in a few days and I'll let him and Amos know." Matthew lifted a humidor from his desk, opened the lid, and asked, "Would you care for a cigar?"

"I don't mind if I do," John took one from the box as Matthew motioned for him to sit.

John lit his cigar and took a few puffs before continuing the conversation. "Koi tells me that your father-in-law, George, might be in some kind trouble."

"I don't know what it could be, but Luther seems concerned."

"Maybe the law thinks he knows something about the Syndicate that might be useful to them. Have you seen the investigators around town lately?

"No. Not for some time. I think my father talks to them now and then since they pretty much stay in Ardmore."

122

John snuffed out his cigar in the onyx ashtray on Matthew's desk. "I think it's time I head back to Okla Chuka. You and the family come see us when you can."

"We'll do that soon," Matthew promised.

John rode back to Okla Chuka, contemplating George's awkward situation. *What does he know that the authorities want to find out?* The question continued to repeat itself over and over in his mind.

◊◊◊

When John arrived at Okla Chuka, he recognized two livery stable horses tied to the hitching post. He rode Fancy to the barn and handed the reins to Ples. "I see we have company."

"Yez, sir, Mr. Prichett. It be those two inspector gentleman," Ples said.

John entered the house through the back door. Rose and Stevetta were in the kitchen making supper.

"Mr. Prichett?" Rose said.

"Yes, Rose?"

"Those inspectors are in the great room, waiting to see you. Miz Koi invited them to stay for dinner."

"Thank you, Rose." John continued on to the great room. Both men stood when he entered.

"Nice to see you again, Mr. Prichett," Frank said.

John shook hands with both inspectors. "Please, have a seat."

"We received your message saying you wanted to talk to us. Sorry it's taken us so long to get back to you," Frank continued.

"No apologies necessary. I just wanted to let you know I made a trip to Bois d'Arc's place not long after you were here last. I spoke with Lawa about his gun."

"Did she say anything that might help us resolve who's murdering people around here?" Lee asked.

"Yes. She told me who killed Francis Kirby."

"Who?" Frank leaned forward, waiting for John to answer.

"Bois d'Arc."

"Bois d'Arc? Did she say why?" Lee jumped in.

"Yes. Kirby cheated one of their sons out of some land, and Bois d'Arc decided it was up to him to take blood vengeance."

"That explains why it looked like the bullet that killed Kirby came from Bois d'Arc's gun," Frank said.

"It doesn't explain who killed Bois d'Arc and who threw his gun in my outhouse." John took a puff from his cigar.

"You're right, it doesn't. One mystery solved, and several more to go before we have all the answers. We intend to get to the root of this criminal bunch and stop this corruption, if it takes us all year." Frank stood to leave and Lee followed suit.

"Won't you be staying for supper?" John asked.

"Not this time. We appreciate your offer, but we've already made arrangements to stay at Fisher's Hotel and boarding house. We'll come back to see you before we leave," Frank said.

John walked the men to the hitching post and bid them goodbye. He had hoped they would say something about George, but they remained silent on that subject. If they had any information, they weren't willing to share it.

◊◊◊

The next afternoon a team of horses pulling a buckboard came charging through the gates and stopped in front of the house. John heard the racket and rushed to see what was going on.

"Mr. Prichett! Mr. Prichett!" one of Osi's wranglers shouted.

"What is it?" John asked as he raced to the wagon. When he peered over the wooden sideboard, he saw a semi-conscience Osi. His body was swollen and his face almost unrecognizable.

"Mr. Nance got bit by a rattlesnake while we were mending fences," the wrangler said.

Everyone in the house had gathered on the porch to see what the commotion was about, and Ples came running from the barn.

"Let's get him in the house," John said.

"Put him in my room." Koi handed Kash to Rose and ran to prepare the bed.

Gentle Woman walked alongside the men as they moved Osi. "Where did it bite him?"

"Near the top of his boot, on his right leg," the ranch hand said. "I tied a bandana above the fang marks to stop the poison from going up his leg, but it doesn't look like it helped. He's all swole up."

"You did good by taking his boots off," Gentle Woman said. She turned to Stevetta. "Go get some hot water and clean rags. Bring them quickly."

As soon as the men placed Osi on the bed, Koi went to his side. She kissed his feverish forehead. "You're home now. We're gonna take care of you and you'll be fine," Koi said gently. Tears streamed down her face and dripped onto his swollen cheeks. "I love you," she whispered in his ear. *Please dear Lord, don't let him die.*

Stevetta came into the room with rags and a pan of hot water. "Is there anything else I can do?" she asked as she sat them on the table next to the bed.

"Just keep water boiling on the stove. I am going to need more than this." Gentle Woman looked up and saw Ples in the doorway. "Go get some mare's milk."

"Mare's milk? We don't have any horses with new foals right now," Ples said.

"I don't care where you have to get it, but we need it now." Gentle Woman spoke with urgency. "Koi, come over here and clean Osi up while I go prepare the things I need to draw out the poison," Gentle Woman ordered.

John had been quietly watching all the activity. Now he took the ranch hand's arm and pulled him from the room. "Thank you for bringing him here as quickly as you did."

"Our cook said to give him some whiskey and that would kill the poison, but I figured it was best to bring him here."

"You did the right thing. Let's go in the kitchen and get Rose to fix you something to eat before you head back to the ranch."

Koi slipped Osi's shirt up and over his head as gently as

125

she could. She washed his face, arms and chest. He moaned and opened his eyes ever so slightly. "You're gonna be okay," she kept reassuring him. Her hands shook so much she had a hard time unbuckling his belt. She pulled his trousers off by jerking his pant legs.

She was washing Osi's injured leg when Gentle Woman returned with the cedar box in her arms. She sat it on the bed and moved forward to examine the site where the rattlesnake fangs had entered his flesh. "That looks pretty nasty," she said. "I'm going to have to cut open his leg. Koi, if you don't think you can handle it, go get Rose to come help," Gentle Woman said.

"No, I'll be fine, Mother."

"All right, let's do it."

Koi stood staring at Osi's leg, holding a damp cloth in her shaking hands. She was prepared to soak up the blood when Gentle Woman cut.

Osi's mother took a razor-sharp obsidian stone from the cedar box and poured whiskey over it to kill the germs. "I wish Ples would get back with that mare's milk," Gentle Woman said. She picked up the glass blade and slashed across the puncture, laying the flesh wide open. Osi flinched and groaned. Blood gushed from the site.

Koi stared in horror, not moving a muscle until Gentle Woman shouted, "Koi! Either wipe this up or give me the rag."

Koi stepped forward and gently wiped the blood from Osi's laceration. Tears welled up in her eyes. Everything looked blurry and she couldn't see what she was doing. She blinked several times, causing a steady stream of tears to run down her face.

Gentle Woman reached for a small brown bottle she had placed on the table and poured the contents into the open wound. Osi moaned loudly. "This is kerosene," Gentle Woman told Koi. "It helps neutralize the poison. It'll do until we can get the Mad Stone on it."

Gentle Woman reached inside her box and took out a packet of ground corn, some snakeroot, a pinch of gun powder, and a small amount of salt. She placed them in a bowl then took an egg from her apron pocket, cracked it open, and dropped the yolk into the mixture. While she stirred the concoction, she

126

ordered Koi, "Go get a plug of tobacco from John."

Koi rushed from the room and swiftly returned, handing the item to Gentle Woman.

"That should do." Gentle Woman pulled off a piece, stuffed it into her mouth and began to chew until it became pliable. She then spit the wad into the bowl with the other ingredients. She mixed the poultice thoroughly and plastered it on Osi's festering flesh. "Hand me a clean rag to bind his leg."

After wrapping his wound, Gentle Woman took an eagle feather from her box. She gently waved the feather across her son's body as she began to pray to Ababinnili.

Chapter Sixteen

Koi dunked a clean rag into cold water and wrung most of the moisture out before placing it on Osi's forehead. His feverish skin felt hot when she kissed his swollen cheek. "Mother, is he going to be all right?"

"It's too early to tell. Let's smudge the room while we wait for Ples to get back with the milk." Gentle Woman pulled a bundle of sage from her cedar box and lit one end. When it erupted in flames, she shook it until the fire went out. The smoking bundle emitted a pungent odor. She fanned the veil of smaze with her eagle feather, making sure every nook and cranny of the room had been reached. She prayed and continued her ceremony while Koi sat in a bedside chair, whispering encouraging words to Osi.

John appeared at the open door. "May I come in?"

"Yes," Gentle Woman said.

"How's he doing?"

"I've done everything I know to do until Ples gets back with the mare's milk." Gentle Woman pulled a chair beside Koi. She picked up Osi's hand and began to gently massage it as she prayed for her son's life.

The back door slammed and Ples rushed in. "Miz Nance. I got what you wanted. I had to go to lots of places before I found some."

"Thank you, Ples." Gentle Woman stood and took the pail. She went to the kitchen and poured part of the liquid into a pan. As it heated to a boil, she went back to Koi's room and retrieved the Mad Stone from her cedar box. She rushed back to the kitchen and dropped the stony concretion into the boiling milk. With a hot pad, she lifted the pan from the stove and took it to Koi's room. "The stone has to soak up some milk before I can use it to draw out the poison," Gentle Woman said.

"While we're waiting, tell me more about the Mad Stone," Koi said. "You've shown me how to use it, but that was a long time ago."

"My stone was taken from the stomach of a white deer. The very best stones come from an albino with pink eyes. It not only cures hydrophobia, but it also cures rattlesnake and spider bites. Always remember that a Mad Stone can never be bought or sold. It must be passed down in families, and one can never charge for its use. When I am gone, you will inherit my Mad Stone, so watch carefully and remember each step."

Gentle Woman unwrapped the bandage on Osi's leg and removed the poultice. The wound had stopped bleeding. She rubbed the flesh with a warm damp cloth until it oozed blood and Osi let out a painful moan. She ignored his cry and continued to instruct Koi. "You have to make sure the area is bleeding or else the stone won't stick and draw out the poison."

"It should be cool enough now." Gentle Woman reached her hand into the warm liquid, retrieved the stone, and gently placed it inside the bleeding cavity. As if by magic, the stone grabbed hold of the flesh and stuck.

"When the stone has soaked up as much poison as it can hold, it'll fall off," Gentle Woman continued. "Then we have to boil and soak it in the milk again. If the milk turns green, that tells us its working and drawing out the poison."

"How many times do we have to this?" Koi asked.

"Until the milk doesn't turn green anymore."

Koi leaned over to take a closer look at the curative stone stuck to Osi's leg.

The brown rock was oval and about three inches long.

"Can I touch it?" Koi asked.

"Yes. Try and shift it with your finger. It's solidly planted. When it has drawn up the poison, it will be easy to move and will eventually fall off."

Koi took the damp rag from Osi's head and freshened it in cool water before placing it back on his forehead. She leaned over and kissed his cheek. "I love you," she whispered and sat down to wait.

The women stayed with Osi throughout the night. It was close to daylight when the stone quit expelling the poison and the milk stayed white.

"That's it," Gentle Woman said when she tried to make the stone stick one last time.

"Mother, he isn't burning with fever anymore." Koi kissed his cheek again.

"Let's get this wound sewn up. We've got him over the pinnacle. If he doesn't get an infection, he will recover."

Osi groaned as his mother stitched his flesh.

Koi continued to talk to him while Gentle Woman worked. "Your mother got the poison out and you're going to be fine. As soon as you're able, we'll go to Pennington Creek for a picnic. Kash can go with us. He loves the creek as much as we do." Koi knew Osi didn't hear her, but she talked anyway.

When Gentle Woman finished, she spoke. "Koi, you need to get to bed. Go sleep in my room. I will rest here in the chair, and when you wake up, you can take over while I go to bed."

Koi nodded, kissed Osi on the lips, and walked from the room.

◊◊◊

The next morning Koi found Gentle Woman and Osi talking. When Osi saw Koi, he smiled and motioned for her to come to him.

"How do you feel?" she asked.

"Like I've been run over by a herd of buffalo."

"He's doing fine, so I'm going to turn his care over to you while I go get some sleep," Gentle Woman said as she left the room.

Before long Rose arrived with a bed tray filled with breakfast for two. "Miz Koi, I figured you'd want to eat here with Mista Nance. I hope y'all are hungry."

"That ham and eggs look wonderful. Thank you, Rose," Koi said.

When Rose left, Koi cut Osi's portion of ham into little pieces. When she stabbed a piece and tried to feed him, he grabbed her hand and took the fork. "I appreciate your help, but I can feed myself," he said.

Koi took her plate and sat down in the chair. "Rose sure does know how to make biscuits," she said.

Osi nodded. When he finished eating, he motioned for Koi to take the tray away.

"You didn't eat much."

"I suppose it'll take me a while to get my appetite back, but I'm always hungry for you." He pulled her to him.

"Osi! Stop that. Someone might hear you!" Koi looked toward the open door.

Osi chuckled.

Koi reached for the hand bell on the table and rang it to summon Rose.

Stevetta appeared in the doorway. "Miz Rose sent me to see if I can help you. She's busy with Masta Kash right now."

"That's fine, Stevetta. You may take the breakfast tray away now. We're finished." Once Stevetta had done as requested, Koi sat back down next to Osi. "You sure gave us a scare last night."

"I don't remember. The last thing I recall is stepping over a log to get to a fence post and feeling an excruciating pain hit my leg. I looked down and there was a big rattler. I was able to kill it before the poison started pumping through me. I hope one of the men took it back to the ranch house to skin. It was at least six feet long,"

"You almost died last night and all you can think about is hoping the men retrieved that snakeskin?" Koi admonished him.

"Well, I'd like to have it to brag with." Osi smiled.

John knocked as he appeared in the doorway. "Good morning, Osi. I see you're looking better than you did when your wrangler brought you here."

"I can't lay around long. I've got a wild west show to prepare for."

"Father, come have a seat and visit with Osi while I check on Kash. I haven't seen him today."

As Koi stepped into the hallway, Osi called from his bed, "Bring him in here, Koi, I want to see him."

"All right," she said.

◊◊◊

Gentle Woman entered the room and saw both men smoking cigars. "Oh, no, you don't!" She took the stogie away from Osi. "You can have this in a few days, but as long as I'm your doctor, you will do as I say." She scowled at John for giving him the cigar.

Osi looked at John and shrugged his shoulders with a sheepish grin. "She's the only person in the world that I let boss me around."

Gentle Woman stepped forward and pulled the covers away from his leg. Examining the wound, she said, "John, I'm going to have to change his bandage, so if you don't want to see this, you better leave the room."

"Okay, I'll be back." John said.

◊◊◊

Later that afternoon the postman delivered a letter. Stevetta placed it on the silver tray in the foyer and forgot about it until she passed Koi and Kash in the hall. "Oh, Miz Cooper, there's a letter for you on the tray."

"Thank you, Stevetta."

Koi let go of Kash's hand and he immediately headed toward the open door to see Osi. Koi didn't bother to catch him; she was eager to read the letter. She ripped open the envelope.

> Dear Koi,
>
> Hope this finds you and the family well. My plan is to leave Chicago as soon as Eli heads for Washington, D.C. That should be in about two weeks. I will send you a telegram notifying you a few days before I get there. If you aren't able to meet me when I arrive, don't fret. I'll be comfortable staying in the train car until you get there.
>
> I am looking forward to this trip to see the Territory and the Wild West Show. I

wish you, Kash, Osi, and the others my
best.

Sincerely,
Claire Dubois
51 East Monroe Street
Chicago, Illinois

Koi folded the letter and placed it in her dress pocket. When she arrived at the bedroom, she saw Kash on the bed and Osi telling him how he got bit by a rattlesnake.

"It was big and had lots of rattles. When you get older, I'll show you how to watch out for them and not get bit like I did. When I get well, we can go to the creek, and I'll teach you how to smell water moccasins."

Koi didn't want to disturb them, so she took a seat next to the bed and stayed quiet until Kash became restless. "Come to me, you little wiggle worm. You're gonna hit his sore leg." She stood him on the floor.

"He's growing up fast," Osi said. "It won't be long until he'll be helping me on the ranch."

"That day will come all too soon for me." Koi picked up the table bell and rang for the help to come get Kash. She wanted to visit with Osi privately. As soon as they were alone, she closed the door. "Osi, I received a letter from Claire Dubois. She's going to come visit us here in the Territory."

"Claire, from Chicago?"

"Yes. I received a letter from her a few weeks ago. She said the senator is going to Washington, D.C., on business, and she's going to use his train car to come to Ardmore. A second letter arrived today. She'll be here in about two weeks but didn't say how long she'd be staying. I told her about the wild west show and that you were going to be participating in it, and she said she wanted to go. The timing for her visit might not coincide with the show date, but with your injury you may not be able to participate this year anyway."

"What do you mean? A little snakebite won't keep me from showing those cowboys how to rope a calf."

133

Chapter Seventeen

Chicago

Claire Dubois sat with Senator Eli Collins in his elaborate white carriage on their way to the Chicago Central Railroad Station. She watched as he caressed the filigree ring on her finger.

When he touched the large emerald, it triggered a bombardment of memories that ran swiftly through her head. A year ago she thought she would be marrying Neville Cooper; instead, he married Koi Prichett. An overwhelming feeling of sadness swept over her as she thought of Neville's death and Osi's trial.

Not wanting to relive the past in her mind, she reverted to her flirtatious self. She pulled her hand away and moved to straighten Eli's collar. She batted her long eyelashes and smiled with a lascivious grin. "You handsome devil."

The senator winked and squeezed her hand as he directed his driver, "My private car is parked alongside the main tracks at Twelfth and Michigan Avenue."

"I am so excited to be going to see Koi. I can't imagine how they live in Indian Territory without the luxuries we have here in Chicago," Claire said.

"The Indians are primitive people. You're going to have to adjust to their ways while you're there. You won't have indoor privacy."

"Are you insinuating I'll be using an outdoor privy?"

"Exactly," the senator grinned.

"In that case, I will be spending most of my time in the train car."

"It's a shame you weren't able to find a suitable maid to accompany you."

"I interviewed several but didn't find any I liked."

"You mean you didn't find any that you wanted to share close quarters with for a month," Eli smiled.

"You are right about that."

"I assumed you wouldn't find anyone to your liking, so I made arrangements with the railroad to ensure luxurious accommodations and care for your ultimate comfort." Eli smiled.

"You are so thoughtful. That's one of the many things I love about you." Claire planted a kiss on his lips.

The carriage stopped alongside the tracks. "This is as close as I can get," the driver said. He secured the horses and began to unload Claire's trunk and suitcases onto a handcart. "Senator, is there any particular place you want the luggage inside the car?"

"Claire can direct you when you get the load delivered," Eli replied. He stood beside the carriage door, ready to help her out of the buggy.

"I hope I didn't forget anything," Claire worried as she grabbed Eli's hand.

"If you did, you probably won't need it in the Territory."

Claire smiled. "Well, I did remember to send a telegram to Koi."

"She won't have a hard time finding you. I've arranged for the train car to be parked close to the depot. It may not be the quietest place, but you'll be around others who can assist you, if necessary."

Okla Chuka

Koi and Gentle Woman had a hard time keeping Osi in bed. The third day after the snakebite, he tried to walk on his injured leg.

"Osi, you better take it easy," his mother said when she saw him hobble to the doorway.

"You know I can't stand layin' in bed."

Gentle Woman pulled a cane-bottomed chair over. "Here, sit," she ordered

"Where's Koi and Kash?" Osi asked.

"They rode to Tishomingo. Koi went to see how Jennie is

fairing with her father's situation with the law."

"Yeah, I'm curious about George too."

"It's time for you to lie back down." Gentle Woman grabbed his arm and nudged him back to bed.

McIvers' Manor

Koi and Jennie sipped tea in the parlor while Etta watched the boys. "Has there been any news about your father?" Koi asked her friend. "The last I heard, Luther was inquiring about legal counsel in case he's charged with some crime."

"Matthew said he and Michael would represent him if the charges amount to anything. My father was always a good man until he got mixed up with those Progressives." Jennie frowned. "He's been a stranger to me in recent years." Her eyes went from her teacup to the bay window when she heard a galloping horse come to a halt near the porch.

"Jennie!" the rider called.

She recognized her brother's voice. By the time she stood and reached for the door knob, he had already opened it and stepped inside. "Father has been missing and no one has seen him for a few days. A posse of men are out looking for him now. I came to Tish' to round up more men to assist in the search."

"When did you see him last?" Jennie asked.

"A couple days ago. I was tending the cows in the back lot when he rode up and said he was going to Ardmore to talk to Michael McIver. When he didn't return at bedtime, I assumed he had decided to stay over."

"Did the investigators charge him with something? Is that the reason he went to talk to Michael?" Jennie asked, nervously clutching her necklace.

"If they had any evidence he committed a crime, they would have arrested him and taken him to jail, but they haven't been to the ranch lately. Before coming here, I went to the law office in Ardmore. Michael said he hadn't seen Father. That's when I became concerned that he never made it there."

Luther turned his head to Koi sitting in the parlor and tipped his hat.

"Come on in and have a seat. Are you hungry?" Jennie asked.

"No, I'm headed to the courthouse. I'm gonna ring the tower bell to round up a posse to look for him between here and Ardmore. My wranglers are looking around Davis and Dougherty. They were searching Sorghum Flats when I left for Tishomingo." Luther turned to leave. "Good day, ma'am." He tipped his hat again to Koi. "I'll let you know when we find him, Jennie." He mounted his horse in a flash and rode toward the courthouse on Capitol Street.

Okla Chuka

Koi bid Jennie goodbye shortly after Luther left, eager to tell everyone at home about George. Before she reached Okla Chuka, the bell on the top of the courthouse began to ring. It could be heard for miles as it tolled for citizens to come for an important message. Luther's continuous ringing denoted the news was neither a death nor a hanging.

Koi reined Bess through the gates and met John as he was leaving. "What's going on?" he asked as he stopped alongside the buggy.

"George is missing. Luther's getting a posse together to go look for him."

"Hmm … Well, I guess I better go see what I can do to help." John rode past the buggy and out the gates.

Koi drove to the barn, handed the reins to Ples, and walked in the back door of the house. "Yoo-hoo, I'm home," she yelled. At her call, Rose came from the kitchen, took Kash from her, and gave him a sweet treat.

Koi slipped off her riding cape and handed it to Stevetta as she walked to her bedroom. When she peeked in the door, she saw Osi standing at the window, looking outside. "What are you doing out of bed?" she asked.

"You know I'm not one to lay around. What's going on in Tish'? The bell keeps ringing."

137

"George Jackson is missing. Luther came to tell Jennie while I was there. He said his father has been gone for a couple of days. George left the ranch to go see Michael McIver in Ardmore, but he never arrived. Luther's rounding up a posse now to go look for him."

"Guess I better get some clothes on and go see what I can do."

"Please don't go, Osi. Let the others look," Koi pleaded.

"Did I overhear you say you're leaving the house? I think not!" Gentle Woman scolded as she walked into the room.

Osi knew it was no use arguing. He sat down in the cane-bottomed chair and pulled Koi onto his lap. "Mother, how about telling Rose to get us something to eat," he said to get rid of her. When she was gone, he turned Koi's face toward his and planted a passionate kiss on her lips.

"Osi, she's liable to come right back," Koi whispered with a smile.

Osi chuckled.

Chickasaw Capitol Building

When John Prichett arrived at the courthouse, a group of men had already gathered on the lawn. They were waiting for the Governor to announce the reason for calling the people to the Capitol.

It wasn't long before Luther came outside and stood on the front steps. With a raised voice he addressed the crowd. "Thank you for coming. My father, George Jackson, is missing. I am here to ask all able-bodied men to join me in a wide search for him between Tishomingo and Ardmore."

Before Luther could say more, a delivery boy stepped up and handed him a telegram. Luther tore open the envelope.

```
TO LUTHER JACKSON
CHICKASAW CAPITOL
TISHOMINGO OKLAHOMA

YOUR FATHER HAS BEEN FOUND DEAD
```

```
STOP
SUICIDE NOTE FOUND STOP

FROM MICHAEL MCIVER
MCIVER ATTORNEY AT LAW
ARDMORE OKLAHOMA
```

Luther crumpled the paper in his hand and without skipping a beat announced that the search has been called off. "My father has been found dead. I don't have any more details."

John Prichett worked his way through the crowd to Luther. "I'm sorry to hear about George."

Luther, still in a state of shock, nodded at John then jumped on his horse and rode toward McIvers' Manor.

Okla Chuka

While John was gone, Osi convinced his mother that he was well enough to go to the great room for a smoke. He was enjoying a cigar when John walked in.

"Are you going to go on the search?" Osi asked.

"Nope. A telegram came from Michael McIver while Luther was gathering the posse. It said George had been found dead."

"Whoa, wonder what happened?" Osi asked.

"Guess we'll find out soon enough. I better tell Koi. I'm sure she'll want to console Jennie."

After John left the great room, Osi continued to sit, puffing his cigar. He blew smoke rings, thinking and waiting for Koi to tell him she was going to be with Jennie.

◊◊◊

Koi spent the night at McIvers' Manor. She and Jennie stayed up, talking, crying, and planning a funeral. Luther also stayed the night at his sister's house. Koi was surprised, since Jennie and Luther had never been close, but with the death of their father, the differences they'd had in the past seemed to dissolve immediately. Matthew welcomed Luther and let him know he was welcome at their home anytime.

◊◊◊

Early the next morning, Michael and Violet McIver arrived at McIvers' Manor. "Let's go in the parlor to talk," Matthew suggested to Michael and Luther. He closed the sliding mahogany doors between the parlor and dining room for privacy.

Jennie, Koi, Violet, and baby Jacob remained at the dining table, eating breakfast.

"I can't believe Jacob has grown so much since the last time I saw him," Violet said. "Let me hold my grandbaby." She reached over and took him from Jennie's arms.

Jennie smiled. She was pleased that Violet had had a change of heart from her old prejudiced ways. It hadn't been that long ago that she'd said she didn't want grandchildren the color of a brown flower pot.

Before long Michael called everyone into the parlor. Violet handed Jacob to Etta then entered the parlor. Everyone took a seat and gave Michael their undivided attention.

"I know all y'all want to know the details," Michael began. "George was found in the Arbuckles by Mr. Price's nephews. They were looking for stray cattle when they came upon George's horse. At the time they didn't know who it belonged to. They were looking for the absent rider when they saw George, hanging by the neck from a tree. They cut him down and took him back to Price Falls. Before they reached the mill, several men rode up and said they were looking for George."

"Why would someone hang our father?" Jennie interrupted.

"No one hung him. He did it himself," Michael said.

"No. It can't be!" Jennie cried.

Michael took a paper from his jacket pocket. "This is the note they found on him." He spoke the words softly:

To my children, Luther and Jennie

*I'm sorry. In order to escape a lengthy trial
and disgrace you both, I chose death.
I am filled with remorse and shame for
killing Bois d'Arc, but I couldn't let him tell
everyone that I have been helping the
Syndicate. There is no other way out.
Please forgive me.*

*Your father,
George Jackson
October 3, 1899.*

Matthew caught Jennie as she fainted. He carried her to the bedroom with Koi close behind. "I can't imagine what she is feeling right now," Koi whispered. She walked to the washstand, wet a cloth, and put it on Jennie's face to bring her around. She stayed with Jennie until the initial shock of losing her father subsided.

"Koi, how could he have killed himself? As Christians we know that's a sin."

Koi didn't answer. All she could do was put her arms around her friend and let her cry until there were no more tears. Koi was glad the others stayed in the parlor and let Jennie handle her grief in her own way.

◊◊◊

"I showed this letter to the investigators before I left Ardmore," Michael said. "Frank said they're awaiting orders from the Commissioner of Indian Affairs. They may leave the Territory and head back to Washington soon. He didn't mention if replacements would be sent or not." Michael took a deep breath and turned to Luther. "Your father's body is at the undertakers in Ardmore. You and Jennie will have to decide where you want him."

"I'm thinking he should be buried in the Tishomingo Cemetery. He'd want to be in the heart of the Chickasaw Nation with his people."

Jennie and Koi returned to the parlor in time to hear Luther's remark.

"I agree. He should be brought back to Tishomingo and buried here," Jennie said.

Chapter Eighteen

George Jackson's funeral came and went. He was quietly buried in the Tishomingo cemetery. The local Methodist minister officiated at the gravesite, giving a nice eulogy. It was a quiet ceremony, with only family and a few close friends attending. Luther and Jennie insisted it be as simple as possible. They questioned how involved their father had been with the Syndicate but were resolved to the fact they might never know. The political differences they'd had in the past seemed to dissolve as soon as their father was in the ground. After the funeral, Luther began to visit McIvers' Manor quite often.

◊◊◊

Two days after George's funeral, the family at Okla Chuka was sitting at the breakfast table when Osi announced, "I'm feeling good now, so I'll be going back to the ranch tomorrow morning. There's a lot to be done before the wild west show."

"I thought you might want to be here when the lumber for the schoolhouse is delivered," Koi said.

"When is it due to arrive?"

"Mark Odell said it would be here in the next day or so," John said.

"I can hardly wait," Koi smiled.

"It's gonna be a mighty fine schoolhouse. The children will have the prettiest teacher in the Territory," Osi grinned.

"You need to stay off that leg for a while longer," Gentle Woman butted in.

Osi ignored his mother. He went to Kash and ruffled his hair. "If I don't get back to work, I'll wither away," he said and walked toward the great room. "John, are you coming to have a smoke?"

"Yes, I'll be there shortly. I need to give Ples some instructions for the carpenters when they arrive."

Koi followed Osi down the hall and took a seat next to him. "Claire should be arriving from Chicago soon. I'm looking forward to showing her around."

"Are you going to bring her to Okla Chuka?"

"Of course, I want her to see where we live."

"Don't bring her to the ranch. The wranglers won't be able to stand that much excitement." Osi winked at her and grinned.

"Are you saying they wouldn't know how to act around a sophisticated lady?"

"That's what I am saying."

"They better hold their hats, 'cause they'll be seeing her at the show."

"When are you going to Ardmore?" Osi asked.

"After I see the lumber delivered. I want to know that it's really happening. When I go I'll stay with Michael and Violet until Claire arrives. Then we'll either stay in the senator's train car or we'll come back here, depending on when the show is held. There are so many places I want her to see."

"Our cave?" Osi asked.

"Only from the creek bank. It's too cold to be climbing over wet rocks." Koi grinned. "And I doubt Claire knows how to swim."

"I have an idea. Let's take Kash and go for a buggy ride around Tishomingo. I'll be leaving in the morning, and it would be nice to spend the day with you two."

"Yes! I'll ask Rose to pack us a lunch."

Osi snuffed out his cigar. "I'll get the rig ready."

◊◊◊

Kash sat on Osi's lap as they rode away from the house. "It's time I taught this boy how to drive," Osi said and showed Kash how to grab hold of the reins.

Koi looked at him and Kash, comparing the shape of their heads, the color of their skin, and the same half-grin. She beamed with pride, imagining her little boy growing up to be the spitting image of his father.

"Penny for your thoughts?" Osi asked.

Koi smiled but didn't reply. It was as if Osi could read her mind.

There was a moment of silence before he tousled Kash's hair and said, "He's my boy!"

They rode along the creek bank. When they reached the cave and whirlpool and Osi stopped the buggy, Kash pointed to the whirlpool and said, "No. No."

"That's right, Kash. That is a no-no place," Koi said.

"Looks like you've brought him here before."

"Of course I have. When we go riding, I often bring him here. This place is special to me. It's where Kash was conceived, you know."

"Hmm …" For a moment Osi was at a loss for words then he grinned. "We might ought to try out that cave again when the weather gets a little warmer."

Koi grinned and tapped him on the arm.

The next morning, after Osi left for the ranch, Koi busied herself packing a trunk to take to Ardmore while waiting for the workmen to arrive with the lumber.

"Rose, I can't decide if I should take a 'Sunday go to meetin' dress or not. I don't think we'll be doing anything that would warrant it, except I know Claire will be wearing one and I don't want her to feel out of place."

"I think you better take that Claire woman to the dry goods store right away and get her some Territory clothes," Rose said.

"I plan to do just that, but I don't know her well enough to know if she'll want to wear what we do."

Rose wrinkled her nose like she smelled something bad. Koi grinned and went back to packing.

Late in the afternoon she heard wagons squeaking and rattling as they bumped over the gravel road. She grabbed her shawl and went to the front porch to wait. When she saw the lumber wagons coming up the drive, she yelled. "Father, the carpenters are here!"

Gentle Woman heard Koi and went to get Kash so he could watch too.

The family, along with the help, watched as a parade of lumber wagons drove past the house to the building site. John, Koi, and Ples went to greet the men while the others went back into the house.

"I sure wish Osi would have stayed to see all these finished planks," Koi said.

"He'll have plenty of time. It's gonna take a while before your schoolhouse is finished."

Koi hugged her father with excitement.

◊◊◊

During next morning's breakfast, a telegram arrived from Claire.

"Oh, my goodness gracious, I need to get to Ardmore as soon as possible." Koi pushed her chair back and stood. "Claire's already there. She says the train made better time than she anticipated."

"I'll tell Ples to ready the buggy." John walked out the back door.

By late afternoon Koi arrived at Osi's ranch. To her surprise he was sitting on the porch smoking a cigar.

"You're a sight for sore eyes," he grinned.

"I came to tell you that Claire's in Ardmore."

"I thought you were going to be there when she arrived."

"I fully intended to be. But I received her telegram this morning saying she was already there."

Osi helped Koi from the buggy. "Come on in. I'll get you something to drink, and I'll tell one of the wranglers to tend to Bess."

"I don't plan to stay long. I need to get to Ardmore as soon as I can."

146

"I won't have you traveling on the road after dark. Claire can wait." Osi pulled her to him and kissed her. "Stay here with me tonight."

Osi's take-charge attitude was hard to deny. It caused the breath to catch in her throat. Somehow she knew this would be a night to remember.

◊◊◊

At daybreak Osi brought the buggy to the front of the house. Koi stood on the porch and waited as he checked the safety of the rig. "I want to make sure there's nothing obvious that might cause you trouble on the road. It looks in fine shape." He rubbed his hand across Bess's mane. "I'll be seeing you in a few days. The show committee is holding a meeting at City Hall and I need to be there."

"Claire and I will either be in the train car or at the McIvers'."

Osi hopped on the buggy step, leaned over, and gave Koi a goodbye peck then stood back to watch as she took the reins and directed Bess toward Ardmore.

◊◊◊

When Koi arrived at the depot, she saw a crowd of people standing around. She wondered what they were doing, and it occurred to her they were looking at the senator's train car. Nothing this elegant had ever been to the Territory that she knew of. She couldn't blame the townsfolk for being curious.

Claire said the senator's car would be parked in plain sight, and there it was, a few yards north of the station. It was a massive object, exuding the wealth and power of its owner. It was a monolith of resplendent polished metal, embellished with a glossy black and gold leaf design running along the entire side of the railcar.

Koi's eyes were drawn from the scrollwork to the roof-fringed metal railing and then to the large vista dome. She had never imagined the senator's mode of transportation would be this luxurious. She took a deep breath, stopped Bess in front of the hitching post near a watering trough, and tied her to the rail. She climbed down from the buggy, walked past the crowd and inside to the ticket counter.

"May I help you, ma'am?" the clerk asked.

"Yes, would you please notify the lady in the private car that Koi Cooper is here?"

"Miss Dubois is expecting you. Please have a seat and I'll get a porter to escort you."

Koi took a seat on an oak bench. Before long a uniformed porter walked up. She followed him through the crowd of people and along the tracks to the rear platform. He stood beside the metal steps with his hand out to help Koi up. Once she was on the platform, he stepped up and rang a small bell hanging outside the door.

"Miss Dubois. Your guest has arrived," he announced.

Claire opened the door and greeted Koi with a bear hug that was totally unexpected. "I'm so glad you're here!"

"Sorry it took me so long. I wasn't expecting you for a few more days."

"That's all right. The train made good time once we got to the Territory. Please come in and make yourself comfortable." Claire turned her attention to the porter. "Please bring us some tea and scones."

"Yes, ma'am, right away."

Koi's eyes surveyed the room. She was awestruck by the opulence. With its ornate, lavish furnishings, the railcar's ambiance was much like that of a deluxe seagoing vessel. She had only seen furniture like this in picture books.

Claire motioned for Koi to have a seat in an overstuffed swivel chair and took a seat across from her. "Now, tell me everything you've done since we last saw each other in Chicago."

"Only if you tell me everything about you and Senator Collins," Koi smiled.

Chapter Nineteen

Claire shifted in her seat. "Life in Chicago with the senator is always exciting. Lately, we have been looking to buy a house. I want a stately mansion downtown, but Eli would prefer something a little simpler. I am sure we will compromise when we find the perfect place. We still have a few months to go before the wedding." The ringing of the platform bell interrupted her. "Excuse me, that must be our refreshments." Claire opened the door and pointed to a table near where she and Koi sat. "Just put it here," she directed.

The porter set the large silver tray down. "Will that be all, ma'am?"

"Yes, that's all for now." Claire turned her attention back to Koi, "Let's see, where were we?"

"You were telling me about house hunting in Chicago."

Koi watched as Claire poured tea into the delicate china cups. "Please help yourself to the scones," Claire said as she handed a cup to Koi.

Koi picked up the silver tongs and lifted a small delicacy onto her crystal dessert plate. "The most exciting news for me lately is the building of a schoolhouse on the grounds of Okla Chuka."

"Okla Chuka?" Claire asked. You mentioned that name in your letter to me.

"Oh, I'm sorry. That's what we call our house. It means 'home of the people' in Chickasaw."

"I can hardly wait to visit your Okla Chuka," Claire said.

"While we're here in Ardmore, I would like for you to meet Violet, Michael McIver's wife. He was the attorney sitting next to Osi during the trial. He came to Chicago and secured the brilliant young defense lawyer who represented Osi."

"Oh, yes, I remember him. He announced the birth of his grandchild at the celebratory dinner."

"I notified Violet that you were coming to the Territory and she wants us to visit her while you're here. Would you like to see her now or should we wait until morning?"

"Let's go in the morning. I'm sure you're tired after driving the buggy all day. I'll ask the porter to bring your things inside."

Koi stood and walked to the door. "I need to make arrangements for the hotel livery stable to take care of my horse and buggy for the night. I'll ask the porter to bring my things inside before I drive to hotel."

The rest of the evening was spent making small talk. At times Koi found it awkward to think of something to say. Claire asked so many questions about Osi, it made Koi uncomfortable. She couldn't understand why Claire was so curious about him.

"I stopped by the ranch on the way here. Osi said he would be coming to Ardmore in a couple days. He's on the wild west show committee and he has to attend a meeting. If we don't go to Tishomingo before he arrives, I'm sure we'll see him here," Koi said.

"I think we should make it a point to stay and greet him." Claire smiled.

◊◊◊

The next day they drove downtown before going to the McIvers' house. The streets were busy with wagonloads of cotton. Koi wove Bess and the little buggy around the horse-drawn vehicles parked in the middle of the street.

"I've never seen anything like this. I thought Chicago was busy," Claire said.

"Ardmore usually isn't this crowded, but it's October and the farmers want to get their cotton to the gins before cold weather sets in."

"What's a gin? I thought that was something to drink." Claire smiled.

"It's a machine that separates the cotton lint from the

150

seeds. After the seeds are removed, the cotton is sent to the compressing plant to be processed into bales."

"That's interesting. It never occurred to me that cotton yardage derives from a plant. I'd like to see it growing."

"There are a few cotton fields between here and Tishomingo. I'll point them out to you when we pass by on our way to Okla Chuka. Picking time is over, but we might be able to see a few bolls left on the dried plants." Koi pointed to a red brick building. "There's the opera house. Occasionally, we get to have a little cultural entertainment."

"You're opening my eyes to a whole new world," Claire said, absorbing all the sights and smells so unfamiliar to her.

Before long Koi turned Bess into a circular driveway. "This is where the McIvers live."

The house was a simple one-story white cottage on stilts with a surrounding covered porch where a swinging bench and two wicker rockers stood.

Koi directed Bess to the hitching post, stepped from the buggy, and flipped the reins over the log rail. She looked back to see Claire trying to get out of the buggy. Claire turned sideways, put her left foot on the step then decided that wasn't going to work. She tried her other foot. Koi walked to her and thrust out a hand to help. All the while, she was chuckling inside. Having spent time in Chicago, Koi knew the buggy steps there weren't as high off the ground as they needed to be in the rough, open spaces of the Territory.

The girls spent the afternoon with Mrs. McIver. Koi was amused at Violet's actions around Claire. She spoke slowly, pronouncing each word methodically, trying to mask her southern accent. "My husband was a judge in Louisiana before coming to Indian Territory," she said.

"That sounds nice. Is Louisiana different than here?" Claire asked.

"Oh, yes! We attended social events and parties. In February, the biggest party of all was Mardi Gras."

"I've heard of it. Do you wish you were still living there?" Claire asked.

"Not now, but when we moved, I was so … homesick. At first I wanted to go back, but you see, my husband likes to drink alcohol and he abused it dreadfully in Louisiana. To keep him from being tempted to stay drunk, we moved here because no alcohol is allowed in the Territory."

"No alcohol?" Claire asked. She stared at Koi, expecting a reply, but Koi just sat quietly, listening to the conversation, a smile on her face.

Violet paused then said. "A person can always go across the river to Texas and get bootleg whiskey, but we don't like to talk about that."

Late that afternoon the women heard footsteps on the porch. "That must be Michael coming home from work." Violet stood to greet him. "Michael, we have guests. Koi is here with Miss Dubois. You'll remember her from your time in Chicago."

"Of course, Miss Dubois, how are you?" Michael thrust out his hand to shake hers. When she didn't respond, he tipped his hat before hanging it on the hall tree. "Will you be staying for dinner?" he asked.

"No," Koi replied. "We didn't notify Violet we were coming to visit. We won't inconvenience you this evening, but we'll take you up on the offer at a later date. Osi is supposed to be coming to Ardmore to attend a meeting in a day or so. I'm sure he would like to join us."

Claire perked up when she heard Osi's name.

Michael smiled. "That'd be good. I haven't had a chance to talk to him since he got bit by that snake."

"Osi got bit by a snake?" Claire asked.

"Yes, but his mother cured him with the Mad Stone," Koi said. "For a while we thought he might not survive."

"Gentle Woman's a good healer, that's for sure. She kept Amos Brooks' son from getting hydrophobia a while back." Michael said.

Claire raised her eyebrows, astonished at what she was hearing. Mad Stone, snakebite, hydrophobia. She wasn't accustomed to this kind of conversation.

"We've taken up enough of your time today." Koi stood and walked to the door. Claire followed. They bid the McIvers good day and promised they'd be visiting again soon.

◊◊◊

The women arrived at the train car as the sun was setting. "I'll let you out here while I take the rig to the hotel livery barn," Koi said. "I won't be long."

"While you're gone I'll order dinner. Is there something you would particularly like?"

"I'm not fussy. Anything is fine for me," Koi answered.

Claire eased out of the buggy, this time remembering how she had done it before. Koi smiled as she watched her walk away with an air about her that screamed "High Class."

Koi turned Bess into the barn and was greeted by a stable boy. She stepped from the buggy and handed him the reins.

"Will you be needin' it again tonight?" he asked.

"No," Koi said. She turned and saw Black Panther in one of the stalls. "Isn't that Mr. Nance's horse?" she asked.

"Sure is. Isn't he a beauty?"

Koi nodded then rushed back to the train car, eager to tell Claire. "Guess who's in town?" Koi yelled, bounding up the platform steps. She opened the door and stopped in her tracks when she saw Osi and Claire facing each other only inches apart with Claire's hand on his shoulder. "Excuse me for interrupting." She shuffled backwards and grabbed the edge of a chair to keep her balance.

Claire's eyes widened when she saw Koi and she quickly stepped away from Osi. "I've convinced him to stay for dinner." She smiled, acting as though nothing had happened, and brushed past Koi, leaving a scented trail of Red Rose by Floris on her way to sit down. "Come join me." She pointed to two close-by chairs.

Koi couldn't help but feel a twinge of jealousy to see the way Osi was being mesmerized by Claire.

Claire focused her attention solely on Osi. She laughed flirtatiously and batted her long eyelashes provocatively at him. She opened a gold inlaid mahogany box on a side table, offered him a hand-rolled cigarette, then took one for herself. She placed hers in a carved ivory holder, but instead of striking a match to light her cigarette, she picked up an engraved silver container. She flipped open the lid, suddenly there was a loud poof, and a tiny flame erupted from the contraption. The small fusee was still burning when she handed the device to Osi after lighting her cigarette.

"What's this thing called?" he asked.

"It's a magic pocket lamp." Claire inhaled deeply and blew the smoke out slowly, focusing her attention on Osi. "Koi said you were coming to town to participate in a Wild West Show. I saw Buffalo Bill Cody's Show in Chicago and it was so exciting. It made the West sound exciting and dangerous. Tell me, what will you be doing in the Show?

Osi laughed. "I doubt our show's going to be anything like the one you saw in Chicago. Those are just entertainment, and they aren't an example of the way we do things here. We'll have a few acts for fun, but our event is mostly a way for cowhands from all the ranches in the region to get together and show their expertise in everything they need to know to be good ranch hands. Calf roping, bronc riding, steer wrestling, and all sorts of skills with their ropes. I'll be entering the calf roping contest."

Koi shifted nervously in her seat. She had seen women smoke tobacco from corncob pipes but never a cigarette or cigar. She sensed Osi was uncomfortable but wondered why he avoided eye contact with her. Her rational mind told her Osi wouldn't fall for Claire's advances, but his actions seemed to be saying something else.

Claire monopolized the conversation over dinner with small talk and tales of her social life in Chicago. She used her eating utensils delicately, as if trying to impress Osi with her sophisticated etiquette.

Koi used her fork to stir the food on her plate. She didn't feel like eating. Her heart was still pounding and she felt nauseous. She had been shaken to her core when she'd seen Osi in a compromising position with the other woman. Claire was a flirt, but Koi had thought it was just her way of being friendly ... until now. She wondered if Claire was the type of woman who needed constant attention from men and would use her charms and any means possible to catch them in her snare.

Osi was hers and hers alone. There was no way she was going to let some catty, highfalutin' woman take him away from her.

Chapter Twenty

Okla Chuka

The day after Koi left for Ardmore, Gentle Woman took Kash outside to play. He was getting to be a handful. His pent-up energy and curiosity kept her busy chasing after him.

Gentle Woman sat Kash down in the front yard grass and took a seat on the porch swing, smiling as she watched him stand and run happily back and forth in his newfound freedom. He went from one hitching post to the other until he tired himself out. It wasn't long before Gentle Woman saw him squatting and poking his finger at something in the grass. She rose from her seat and went to see what he was doing.

"See? See?" Kash said, pointing to an object in the grass.

"Oh, my, what do you have there?" Gentle Woman asked. She saw that it was a baby terrapin. "*Loksi*," she said in Chickasaw. "Kash, can you say *loksi*?"

He attempted to say the word, but it came out, "Loosi."

"That was a good try," she said. "*Loksi*, that's what we call this kind of turtle."

She picked up the terrapin with one hand and lifted Kash onto the porch with the other. "Let's take him to the swing and I'll tell you a story about another little *loksi* that lived a long time ago."

"Want loosi," Kash said, reaching for the turtle.

"All right, let's get seated first." Once Kash sat down, Gentle Woman placed the small terrapin in his lap. He grabbed the turtle, ready to throw it across the porch, but Gentle Woman caught his arm. "That isn't nice. You be kind to the little

155

creature," she scolded him. She took his hand and guided it gently across the turtle's shell. "See, this is a good *loksi*."

Kash began to gently pet the small creature.

"Once upon a time, some naughty boys found a terrapin in a strawberry patch. They were mean boys and weren't kind to animals. They hit the *loksi* with sticks until they broke his shell. They left him crying in pain and unable to move. A nest of gnats heard his cry and came to help. They saw his cracked shell and knew they needed to mend it. Seeing a layer of orange-colored, hair-like thread covering some nearby weeds, they gathered it and used it to sew the terrapin's wounds together. The *loksi* soon healed, but to this day he carries thirteen cracks on his back."

Gentle Woman drew her finger around each segment, showing Kash the lines. "Next time we see orange hair growing on the grass, I'll point it out to you. We call it Loksi's thread." Gentle Woman knew Kash didn't understand nor would he remember what she told him, but she would repeat it many times over the years.

She lifted Kash and the terrapin from the swing. "Let's take Loksi in the house and see if Rose has something we can put him in. You can keep him until your mother gets home. Afterwards, we'll let him loose so he can go home to his mother."

Ardmore—the Train Car

"Thank you, Miss Dubois, for the lovely meal. I hope you will accept my apologies for leaving early, but I don't want to arrive late at the McIvers' house." Osi stood and walked to the door.

Koi went to his side. She waited for him to give her a hug. Instead, he stepped away from her without making eye contact. It was Osi's nature not to show affection in public, but after the incident with Claire, Koi thought he would at least give her some kind of reassurance that he loved her.

"I'll be going back to the ranch after the meeting tomorrow and probably won't see y'all until the show." Have fun in Tishomingo." He walked out the door.

Koi felt a lump in her throat. It was all she could do to keep from crying.

"You're as white as a sheet. Are you all right?" Claire asked.

"I'm fine." Koi had just turned to sit down when she lost consciousness and slumped to the floor.

Claire quickly rang for the porter. While she waited for help, she held a damp cloth to Koi's forehead and repeated, "Wake up! Wake up!"

Before the porter arrived, Koi regained awareness of her surroundings. "I'm sorry," she said softly. When she tried to sit up, she was overcome by nausea and weakness. "I don't know what's wrong with me," she said.

"Lie still. When the porter gets here, he can help you to the bed, and I'll ask him to call a doctor," Claire ordered.

"No, please don't call a doctor. I'll be fine with a good night's sleep." Koi managed to get into bed without the help of the porter. She tried to drift off, but she hardly slept. Her mind replayed the scene of Claire and Osi over and over. She tossed and turned all night, and it was daybreak before she finally fell asleep. It seemed as if she'd only been asleep for a few minutes when she was awakened by someone ringing the platform bell.

"That must be our breakfast," Claire mumbled. "Just a moment!" she yelled to let the porter know she would be there shortly. At the door to the car, she took the tray from the porter, sat it on a table, and went back to bed.

The smell of freshly brewed coffee, maple-cured bacon, and scrambled eggs emitted a mixed aroma that permeated the entire train car. Most mornings this would have been inviting, but today it was disgusting to Koi. She tried burying her head in the down pillow to keep from smelling the food, but before long she was frantically searching for something nearby to throw-up in. A washbasin and a pitcher stood within arm's reach. She raised her head from the pillow and heaved profusely, projecting bile into the bowl.

"I think we need to call the doctor. You are having serious intestinal distress," Claire said.

"No, no, I'll be okay." Koi took a hand towel from the washstand, dampened it in the pitcher of water, and used the

157

cloth to wash her face and wipe her mouth. "I really want to go home. Gentle Woman will know what to do for my sickness."

"We can't go until you feel like making the trip," Claire said.

"The road from Ardmore to Tishomingo has improved lately. If we leave early we might be able to travel without stopping for the night. We can stay over at Greasy Bend Inn if we have to," Koi said.

The next morning the women left Ardmore before daylight. Claire's luggage weighed down the buggy, causing Bess to struggle to get it moving along the road. Koi had asked Claire to leave some of her things behind in the train car, but she had insisted on bringing her entire wardrobe.

The brisk October air seemed to refresh Koi. She felt pretty good that day but wasn't in any mood to talk. Instead, she kept her eyes on the road and drove Bess at a slow, steady pace. When Claire asked her questions, she answered sharply and didn't elaborate.

Claire sensed a strange coldness about Koi, but she attributed it to her illness. It never occurred to her that she was the cause of Koi's standoffishness. "Koi, I believe nature is calling. When will we be near a water closet?"

Koi directed Bess to the side of the road, stopped, and pointed to a weed-filled culvert. "That's a good spot."

Claire looked at her wide-eyed. "You mean I have to relieve myself in those weeds?"

"That's as good a place as any," Koi said.

Claire clumsily exited the buggy. She lifted her layered skirts and stepped gingerly through the Johnson grass. She tiptoed along the edge, trying to find the perfect place to squat. Finally, she hiked her skirt and petticoats into a bundle and held them to her side. With her free hand, she tried to pull down her bloomers.

Koi felt a perverse sense of satisfaction seeing her struggle. She watched Claire crouch with only her head showing above the surrounding vegetation. In an instant, Claire bounced back up, screaming. She tried to run but stumbled over her undergarments and tumbled down into the ditch, still screaming. "Help me! There's a snake!"

Koi turned her head in the opposite direction, trying to gain her composure. She wiped the Cheshire Cat-like grin from her face before she looked again at Claire. "A little snake won't hurt you; it's as scared of you as you are of it," Koi yelled.

Claire crawled on her hands and knees until she got to a place where she could stand. She hobbled back to the buggy with her bloomers down around her ankles, leaving a trail of liquid behind her.

"It's time you bought some Territory clothes," Koi said. "We wear bloomers with a slit in the crotch for times like these."

Claire stood beside the buggy, took off her wet clothes, and held the dripping garments in her hands, not knowing what to do with them.

"Just stuff them in the back with the luggage. We'll be at Okla Chuka before long and Rose can clean them for you," Koi said.

They passed Osi's ranch just as the sun was setting. Koi knew he would be there and hoped he was still in the north pasture and not on the porch to see them go by. They sailed smoothly past the ranch without anyone in sight. Koi didn't tell Claire that Osi lived there. She felt the less said about him the better.

Koi was determined to get home if she had to drive all night and it was long after dark when they pulled into the drive at Okla Chuka. She drove directly to the barn.

"You're getting home awful late, Miz Koi," Ples said as he hurried from the bunkhouse.

"We are, and it sure feels good to be home." Koi stepped from the buggy and handed Ples the reins. "Bess needs a rub-down. She's had quite a workout, pulling this heavy thing."

Claire exited her seat and walked to where Koi stood.

"This is our house guest, Miss Claire Dubois from

159

Chicago," Koi introduced her.

"It's a pleasure to meet you, ma'am," Ples said.

Claire nodded. She felt very much out of place and wished she had never decided to visit the Territory.

"Ples, you can unload the buggy in the morning. We'll manage just fine tonight without our luggage."

"Excuse me, Koi. I need clean clothes and my toiletries."

"I have a nightgown you can wear. It's late and we're not going to burden Ples with it tonight."

They walked in the back door. Everyone was in bed and the house was dark. Koi fumbled until she found a lantern. "Follow me down the hall. I'll show you to the guest room and get you a nightgown." She opened the bedroom door and placed the lamp on a table next to the bed. "There's water in the pitcher," she said, pointing to the washstand. "Inside the double doors beneath is a chamber pot if you need to relieve yourself."

Claire stood in the middle of the room, trying to decide what to do first.

Koi returned shortly with a silk gown and robe that she tossed across the bed. "Here you go. I'll see you in the morning." She walked out and closed the door.

◇◇◇

Koi was relieved to be home. She walked to her bed and plopped across the top of the quilt. Her clothes were dirty and she needed to wash up, but she was too tired to care. She went to sleep almost immediately.

◇◇◇

At daybreak a crowing rooster startled Claire awake. It took a few minutes for her to realize she was at Okla Chuka. She tried to go back to sleep, but the rooster wouldn't let her. She tossed and turned, wondering what kind of surprises this day would bring.

Chapter Twenty-One

Koi awoke to the sound of Kash's voice coming from the hallway. "Show Mama Loosi."

"Shh … we need to let her sleep. You can show her when she gets up," Gentle Woman said. She ushered him away from the door.

◊◊◊

The familiar sounds at Okla Chuka gave Koi comfort. She lay still, listening to the carpenters hammer the studs for her schoolhouse. She had a moment of elation before reality set in: she was still nauseous. She reached for the chamber pot and heaved several times before the feeling subsided. She wiped her mouth and washed her face. Her thoughts wandered to Claire. *Was she still sleeping?* Having no idea what time it was, Koi opened her door, looked down the hall, and called, "Rose?"

"Yes, Miz Koi?" Rose scurried toward her.

"Please come inside. I need your help."

Rose stepped into Koi's room, closed the door behind her, and stood, waiting for instructions.

Koi sat on the bed, trying to get her thoughts together. "What time is it?" she asked.

"It's afternoon, ma'am. 'Bout two o'clock."

"Afternoon? Is Miss Dubois up?"

"Yes, ma'am. We's already had our dinner."

"Did you and Stevetta meet Miss Dubois?"

"Yes, ma'am," Rose answered. "Masta Kash has been waitin' for you to wake up. He's got somethin' he wants to show you."

"Tell him I'll be out to see him as soon as I can change these dirty clothes." She went to her chifferobe, opened the double doors, and pulled out her red calico dress. She held it close. Her sensitivity to smell was heightened when she caught a faint whiff of something that reminded her of Chicago and the trial. She didn't want to be reminded of Chicago. She held the dress in both hands and flipped it in the air to fan away all the memories before changing into it.

When Koi stepped into the hallway, all she could hear was Kash chattering from the parlor. She peered into the room to see Gentle Woman knitting and Kash playing with something on the floor.

"What have you got there, Kash?"

"Mama!" He ran to her, took her by the hand, and led her to his surprise. "Loosi!" he said.

"It sure is. That's a cute little *loksi*." Koi picked up the small creature and held it gently in her hands. "Where did you find him?" Kash pointed to the front yard and Koi smiled as she remembered playing with turtles when she was a child.

Gentle Woman sat her knitting in a basket and stood up. "You look kinda peaked. Are you feeling all right?"

"Yes, I'm fine. I must've caught something while I was in Ardmore, but I'm better today," Koi mumbled.

"I told Kash he could keep the turtle until you got home. It's time we turn him loose." Gentle Woman picked up the terrapin with one hand and led Kash out the door with the other.

Koi walked toward the kitchen but stopped when she overheard Rose and Stevetta talking.

"That Miz Dubois thinks she's better than ever'body else. Did you see the way she showed off in front of Mista Nance? She was all gussied up, flipping her hair and batting her eyes at him. It was downright shameful." When Rose turned and saw Koi in the doorway, the chatter stopped and all was silent.

"Did I hear you say Osi was here?"

"Yes, ma'am," Rose said.

Stevetta continued to shell peas and pretended to be oblivious to the conversation.

"Where's Osi now?" Koi asked.

"Since you wasn't up to show Miz Dubois around, he took her for a ride in the buggy," Rose said.

"What?" Koi's heart sank and she stumbled backward a few steps before regaining her balance. "Did they say where they were going?" she asked.

"No, only that they'd be back for supper."

◊◊◊

Koi grabbed a cold biscuit from the pie safe and walked out the door. She headed to the construction site to find her father talking to the carpenters.

"Well, good morning, Sunshine," he said.

Koi wanted to be interested in the progress of her building, but at the moment her racing mind wouldn't let her think of anything except Osi and Claire. She turned and threw the biscuit into some bushes on her way back to the house.

"Hey, where are you going? Don't you want to take a walk-through?" John asked.

"Not now, Father," she said and continued to the house. She let the screen door slam when she entered. "Rose, Stevetta, I'm not feeling well. I'm going to my room and don't want to be disturbed."

"Yes, ma'am," Rose replied.

Koi closed her door and threw herself spread eagle across her bed. She buried her head in the down pillows and cried herself to sleep.

◊◊◊

It was after dark when Koi awoke. She heard voices in the great room. Osi's deep cadence resonated throughout the house. The next sound she heard was Claire's unmistakable silly giggle. Koi roused herself off the bed and walked to the great room. There sat Claire, smoking a cigarette in her fancy holder. She was sitting in one of the straight back chairs directly in front of both men. As Koi watched, she lifted her cigarette and said, "This one contains tobacco with an essence of cherry and a hint of menthol. It's one of my favorites."

"You sure know your tobacco, Miss Dubois," John said.

Koi could see they were enamored with Claire's knowledge of tobacco and didn't notice when Koi appeared in the doorway. She cleared her throat. "Ahhh … excuse me, I hope I'm not interrupting anything."

John and Osi both jumped to their feet to stand while Koi walked into the room. However, they quickly sat back down again and returned their attention to Claire.

"Oh, Koi," Claire said. "I hope you're feeling better. Osi was so kind to entertain me today while you were recuperating. He's such a marvelous host. He took me to Pennington Creek. Such a charming place. I can understand why you find peace and tranquility along its banks."

Claire continued to talk until Koi wanted to scream, but she managed to hold her emotions in check and swallow her tears. "I am sorry I missed the fun." Koi's remark was cordial, but her stiff body language said something else. An uncomfortable wave of silence swept over the room.

Osi stood to leave. "I'm going to bid y'all goodnight. I've got business to take care of early, so I'll say farewell now and see y'all at the show."

Koi was miffed at Osi actions. He seemed so preoccupied with Claire that he hadn't even noticed she was wearing his favorite dress. Always before Osi had been quick to compliment her, but tonight it was as though she didn't exist.

◊◊◊

Koi tossed and turned all night. One nightmare morphed into another. By the time she awoke the next morning, she was exhausted. She didn't want to face Claire, so she quickly dressed and slipped out the back door. "Ples, I'm going to town and need you to saddle Cricket," she said when she found him in the barn.

"Yes, ma'am."

She rode straight to McIvers' Manor. Jennie had been her confidant since they were children, and hopefully, now she could give her insight as to what was happening to tear her world apart.

Koi threw Cricket's reins over the hitching post in front of Jennie's house and bounded up the porch steps. She knocked and Etta answered the door.

"Mrs. Cooper, please come in," Etta said.

"I'm here to see Jennie. Is she available for company this early?" Koi asked.

"She's not home, ma'am. They went to Ardmore yesterday to see family. I'm the only one here right now," Etta said.

"Oh. When are they expected back?"

"They said something about staying until the wild west show's over."

"Well, then, I suppose I'll have to see her in Ardmore." Koi frowned and walked away. She rode home by way of the creek, thinking this might be the best way of quieting the noises in her head, but the rippling waters trickling across the granite boulders did nothing but bring back memories that made her want to cry. The one thought that kept playing over and over was one of desperation. *What if I'm with child?*

Koi took Cricket to the stable and handed her over to Ples. By now the carpenters had arrived for the day and were hammering away on the schoolhouse. She walked to the construction site, observing every detail. The thought of teaching school wasn't as exciting as it had been just a few weeks ago.

As a teacher she was supposed to be a role model for the students. How could she face the embarrassment of having a child without being formally wed? Her thoughts turned to her father and how ashamed he would be that she would tarnish the family name.

Koi was tired of thinking, but her mind would not shut up. She walked back to the house to find everyone having breakfast at the kitchen table. Kash sat next to Gentle Woman, jam smeared across his face. Koi patted him on the head and took her seat.

Claire was monopolizing the conversation, but immediately fell silent when Koi walked in.

"Where have you been so early this morning?" John asked.

"I went to see Jennie. I didn't realize they had already gone to Ardmore."

"I guess I'll have to wait to meet your friend when we go back to Ardmore," Claire said.

Koi sat down and buttered a biscuit. Before she could take a bite, however, she was overcome by nausea. "Excuse me, but I feel the need to lie down." She stood and retreated toward her bedroom.

"When you're feeling better, come to the parlor, I'd like to talk to you," Gentle Woman called down the hall.

◊◊◊

Koi tapped her knuckles on the parlor doorjamb to let Gentle Woman know she was there.

"Come on in, Koi," Gentle Woman said, pointing to a nearby chair. "Are you ready to tell me what's wrong?"

Koi buried her face in her hands. "I think you know," she mumbled.

"If you're referring to the reason you're sick, then yes, I know. That's unmistakable."

"Then what are asking me about?"

"You're not treating your company very nicely. Claire has come a long way to visit with you, yet you barely give her the time of day."

"Mother, I feel so threatened by her. She demands Osi's attention, and I'm afraid he's falling for her."

"Koi, jealousy doesn't become you. You need to snap out of it and be the gracious hostess you've always been."

"But, Mother, Osi won't look at me," Koi said.

"Your emotions are running rampant. I'm sure there's some reasonable explanation for your overreaction to Claire's friendly gestures. Maybe Osi's trying to make up for your rudeness. She won't be here much longer. You need to make the best of it and let her leave on good terms. I suggest the two of you go to town. You can introduce her to Territory clothes so she'll be more comfortable on the drive back to Ardmore."

Gentle Woman had a calming effect on her and Koi sat still, letting the present conversation sink in before going to the older woman. She gave her a peck on the cheek. "Thank you, Mother, for grounding me. I'll do my best to be polite."

Chapter Twenty-Two

Claire sat on the porch swing, thinking about the past few days. When she had been in Chicago, she had wanted to come to the Territory, but now she questioned if she had made a mistake. Koi hadn't made her feel welcome. She tried to excuse Koi's strange behavior because she was sick, but it was getting harder and harder for her to tolerate. She was ready to go home.

Just then Koi walked out onto the porch. "Claire, I'm feeling much better. Let's go to town and get you some Territory clothes."

Claire smiled and stood. "Give me a minute to freshen up, and I'll be ready to go."

"I'll get the buggy and meet you here."

Claire rushed off while Koi went to the stable to get Bess and the buggy.

Koi's talk with Gentle Woman had given her much to think about. She realized her jealousy was caused by her own insecurity, and if Osi was smitten with Claire, there was nothing she could do about it. Her inner strength gave her power, and she knew she could endure this crisis. From this moment on she would pretend nothing had happened between Osi and Claire.

All the way to town the women giggled and joked like school girls. Koi drove Bess to the Harris General Store on Capitol

Street. Several men were seated in straight-back wooden chairs facing each other at the entrance. They were smoking and in deep conversation when the women pulled up.

"What are those men doing?" Claire asked.

"Oh, they like to sit, and *shoot the breeze* as my father would say."

All eyes were on the women when they exited the buggy. "Good day, Mrs. Cooper. How's your father today?" one of the men asked.

"He's just fine, Mr. Harris." Koi stepped inside the store, with Claire close behind. A dark-skinned woman stood behind a counter. "Hello, Nellie, I brought my friend Miss Dubois, from Chicago, to buy some clothes," Koi said.

"You came to the right place. What items are you looking for?"

"She needs some bloomers and anything else you think she might need." Koi smiled.

"I can fix her right up." Nellie turned and lifted a cardboard box from one of the shelves. "I think these are your size. Look through this box while I see what else I can find."

Claire took the lid off the box and lifted out a pair of bloomers. She quickly let them drop back into the box, looking around to see if any of the men were watching. She kept the article in the box while she fumbled to see if there was a slit in the crotch. There was. "Yes, I'll take these," Claire said.

While Nellie showed Claire several riding habits, Koi stood at a counter across the room, looking at a new batch of gloves.

Claire liked everything Nellie brought out. "Koi, look!" She modeled a large-brimmed straw hat, turning her head to the left then to the right. "I think I need this to keep the sun off when we travel back to Ardmore."

"It looks nice on you," Koi said.

"I'll take it." Claire handed it to the clerk and Nellie placed it on top of the pile of clothing Claire had already chosen. "Koi, do you think I need some boots?"

"Only if you think you'll wear them."

Nellie sat several boxes of high-topped women's boots on the counter for Claire to look through.

"Oh, look at these," Claire lifted one of the boots from the box. "I love these. I've never seen boots this shade of maroon, and look at the tiny glass buttons," Claire said. "If they fit, I'll take them."

"There's a pair of gloves in this case the same color. You ought to come take a look," Koi called from across the room. Claire walked over to see Koi pointing to the pair of matching gloves. "May I please try these on?" Claire asked Nellie.

"Certainly." Nellie opened the glass case and handed them to Claire.

Claire looked them over thoroughly and slipped one hand into the soft kid leather. "Yes! These are perfect! I'll take them."

Koi smiled at her friend's enthusiasm. "We're gonna have to take two buggies to Ardmore to get all your belongings back to the train car."

Nellie began the task of wrapping Claire's purchases. She took one item at a time to a separate counter where a roll of brown paper and a ball of twine were kept. She meticulously wrapped and tied each article into a bundle and stacked them near the register.

"Claire, I think you bought the entire stock of women's articles," Koi said.

Claire smirked. "Ha. I'll have fun showing all this to Eli." She leaned over, winked, and whispered to Koi, "He'll especially like the bloomers."

Koi was surprised Claire was so brazen as to say Eli would like the split crotch, but she couldn't hold back a small giggle that erupted in her throat. She knew exactly what Claire was thinking.

When Nellie finished wrapping Claire's purchases, she walked to the door. "Would any of you mind carrying Miss Dubois's purchases to the buggy?"

All the men stood at once, but before they could move, a boy about ten years old bolted to the door. "I can do it, Miz Nellie."

Nellie nodded and he followed her inside. While the boy loaded the buggy, Nellie tallied the price of each item in a ledger book. The list took up several pages. When she finished adding the cost, she handed it to Claire to look over. Without hesitation,

Claire opened her ridicule and pulled out several gold certificates. "Keep the change for your trouble," she said as she handed them over.

"I'm much obliged, ma'am. Thank you, very much."

◊◊◊

Bess trotted all the way to Okla Chuka with Claire's packages stacked high. When Koi turned Bess in at the gates, they saw everyone from the household standing on the front porch.

"I wonder what's going on," Koi said. She directed Bess to the hitching post and yelled. "What's going on?"

"Come see," John offered.

Koi and Claire stepped from the buggy and rushed to see what all the excitement was about. Smiling, Kash moved from behind Ples, holding a fuzzy white ball of fur. "Mama, Nashoba Toby," Kash yelled.

"Where did you get that beautiful dog?" Koi asked when she took the puppy from him.

"Papaw," he said.

"He liked that little turtle so much, I thought it was time this boy had a dog," John said. "Every young man needs a dog."

"He's so cute!" Koi petted and stroked the animal before handing him back to Kash.

Claire stepped forward. "May I see your puppy, Kash?" The little boy proudly held Nashoba Toby so Claire could touch him. "Is someone going to tell me why you named him that strange name?" Claire asked.

"Oops. I forgot you don't speak Chickasaw. Nashoba is our word for dog or wolf and toby means white," Koi explained. "That's a perfect name. White Wolf," Claire remarked.

"I think we should call him Toby for short," John said.

"Miz Koi, would you like for me to unload the buggy before taking her to the stable?" Ples asked as he walked over to pet the ever-patient Bess.

"Yes, please. You can put the packages in Claire's room." Koi turned to Claire, waiting for her nod of approval.

"Looks like you bought out the store," John said when he

171

RETURN TO OKLA CHUKA

saw all the packages.

"She just about did," Koi replied with a smile.

Claire fidgeted and her cheeks blushed before she spoke. "Well, there were so many nice things I can't buy in Chicago, and I don't know when I will be coming back to the Territory."

"I'm sure Mr. Harris appreciated your business," John said. "Let's celebrate Toby's addition to the family. Rose, please bring us some lemonade."

"Yes, sir, Mr. Prichett."

Rose and Stevetta turned and walked to the kitchen. Ples made several trips to Claire's room before all the packages were unloaded. When the buggy was empty, he drove Bess to the stable.

Koi and Claire took a seat on the porch swing, John sat in his large wicker porch chair, and Gentle Woman helped Kash and his puppy down the steps to the front yard.

Taking a seat next to John to watch the two little ones play, Gentle Woman said, "That boy is growing up too fast."

"He sure is. It wasn't that long ago that Osi and Koi were his age," he reminisced.

Kash giggled when Toby licked his face. They romped back and forth across the yard while the adults enjoyed their lemonade. Then everyone looked toward the gates when they heard hoofbeats coming down the road.

Osi, riding Black Panther at full speed, abruptly stopped at the hitching post and slid out of the saddle in one swift movement. He went immediately to Kash and Toby. He sat down on the grass and motioned for Kash to come to him. Excited to see him, Kash ran into his arms with Toby at his heels. Osi squeezed him in a bear hug, and they rolled over and over in the grass.

Koi was surprised to see Osi. He had said he wouldn't see them until the show in Ardmore. She couldn't understand why he would be coming to Okla Chuka now. A thought ran through her mind that maybe his fondness for Claire drew him there. She quickly squelched that idea because she didn't want to cry. Watching Osi play with Kash wreaked havoc with her emotions. She took her handkerchief from her pocket and wiped away a stray tear, hoping no one saw.

Osi let go of Kash and the boy was on his feet almost immediately, running after Toby. "Where did you get that puppy?" Osi asked.

Kash continued to chase after his dog and didn't answer, so John answered for him. "I bought it for him. I figured it was time he had a companion."

Osi stood and brushed the dried grass off his clothes. He stepped onto the porch and went directly to his mother. He gave her a peck on the cheek then turned to Koi and Claire. "Good afternoon, Claire," he said.

Koi looked away and stared blankly into space while her heart broke into pieces.

"I came to tell y'all the show date has been moved up. It'll be held on Saturday."

"That's two days from now. It sure doesn't give us much time to get ready. I suppose we need to leave tomorrow," John said.

Osi turned to Koi. "I'd like to talk to you privately." By now her heart was pounding so hard she thought the others could hear it. Osi motioned for her to come indoors. Koi stood, but her knees were so weak she didn't know if she could walk. She slowly followed Osi to the parlor and he closed the door.

As Koi walked across the room to sit, she became light-headed. She took a deep breath and then lost consciousness.

Osi caught her before she hit the floor. He swooped her up in his arms and carried her to her room, laid her on the bed, took a cloth from the washstand, dipped it into the pitcher of water, and placed the wet rag on her forehead. "Koi, what's wrong?" he asked. He took her hand and gently patted it. "Tell me, please!"

Osi was not one to lose his composure, but seeing her like this frightened him. He leaned over and kissed her on the lips.

Koi opened her eyes to see him hovering over her. For an instant she was confused and had no idea what had just happened. Then she remembered Osi wanting to talk to her. She panicked and tried to sit up, but Osi quickly embraced her and held her tightly, rocking back and forth.

173

"You sure gave me a scare," he said, continuing to cradle her in his arms. "All I wanted was to ask you a question. When can we get married?"

"You weren't going to tell me you were in love with Claire?"

"Of course not! What would ever give you that idea?" Osi wrinkled his brow.

"You mean you aren't smitten with her?"

"No. You are my one and only."

Koi put her arms around him and kissed him passionately.

"Before this leads to something else, are you going to tell me when we can get married?" Osi asked.

"I thought we were going to wait until December. That's when it would be a year since Neville's death," Koi said.

"Claire has convinced me we should do it now while she's here. She wants to host the wedding in the senator's train car."

"That doesn't give us time to plan. She'll probably leave for Chicago soon after the festivities." Koi said.

"All the better," Osi grinned. "Her bossy personality is starting to get on my nerves. From the first day she arrived, she's been pushing me to ask you and set a date.

Koi planted another kiss on his lips. "I became your wife when we had our traditional ceremony, but now it will be officially recorded."

Osi slid onto the bed next to her and pulled her close. They lay quietly side by side in a state of bliss, not uttering a sound.

Chapter Twenty-Three

John shuffled his feet and stood. "It sure is taking them a long time to discuss their private business. It must be mighty important." He looked in Claire's direction and saw a smirk dart across her face.

"It's almost time for supper. We better get cleaned up before Rose tells us it's on the table." Gentle Woman went to the yard to round up Kash and Toby. She lifted the dog with one arm and with the other she led Kash onto the porch.

"Here, I'll take him," John reached for the puppy. "Ples can keep him in the stable until we can get a doghouse built."

When John took Toby from Gentle Woman, Kash yelled and tried to grab his playmate. "Nashoba Toby!"

"You can play with him tomorrow. It's time to get ready for supper," Gentle Woman promised as she pulled him in the house.

◇◇◇

Claire walked to the door. When she stepped inside, she saw Koi and Osi holding hands as they walked down the hall. "We were beginning to wonder what happened to both of you," she teased.

"We had important things to discuss," Koi snuggled closer to Osi. "He told me you want us to get married while you're here."

"Yes, that's true. I've been working on it."

Koi smiled. "We've decided to accept your offer."

"Oh, I was hoping you would. Have you decided when?" Claire asked.

Koi looked at Osi and waited for him to respond.

"The sooner, the better," he said. He squeezed her hand gently before letting go. "You girls have some planning to do. I think I'll go have a smoke with John before dinner."

◊◊◊

Midway through the evening meal, Osi stood and clinked his spoon on his water glass. "I have an announcement to make." He looked at Koi and smiled. "We've decided to get married in the senator's train car while Claire is here."

"It's about time," John said then added without skipping a beat, "We have to leave for Ardmore first thing in the morning if we expect to be there on time. We should start packing as soon as we're finished eating."

Osi pushed his chair back from the table and stood. "I better get going. My men are probably already in Ardmore with the stock."

"If you leave now, you'll have to ride all night," Koi protested. Her expression begged him to stay.

"Sorry, Koi. I need to get going so I'll have time to practice."

"I'm thinking we should stay at the hotel rather than with the McIvers, since there will be so many of us," John stated.

"That's a good idea. It will be easier to handle Kash at the hotel," Gentle Woman said. "He's so rambunctious. I worry about him breaking something at the McIvers' house."

Osi walked to the door. "I'll be staying with the men at the campgrounds, but I'll be driving by the hotel. Do you want me to make reservations for y'all?"

"Yes, please do." John looked at Koi. "Do you need a room or are you going to stay with Claire?"

"She'll be staying with me," Claire said. "We have lots of planning to do."

Koi nodded.

"Okay, you better make reservations for three, plus a place for Ples and Rose. We'll leave Stevetta here to hold down the fort," John said.

Koi walked outside with Osi. "You've made me the happiest woman in the world."

Osi pulled her close and kissed her before swinging into the saddle. He took the reins and turned Black Panther toward Ardmore. "I'll see you day after tomorrow."

◊◊◊

Koi slowly walked back into the house, her mind running a million miles a minute.

Claire was waiting for her by the back door. "Have you thought about what you're going to wear at your wedding?" she asked.

Koi didn't have to think about it. She knew exactly what she would wear. "I'll wear my red calico."

"I thought maybe you would want to buy a new dress in Ardmore."

"No, I prefer it be a simple affair with only close friends."

"Do you want the ceremony before or after the show?"

"I'd prefer after. It'll be over before dark, and we can go directly to the train car," Koi said.

◊◊◊

Details of the wedding continued to flash through Koi's mind in rapid succession. She tugged on a lock of hair to make sure she wasn't dreaming. As she moved at a fast pace down the hall with Claire at her heels, her thoughts bombarded her with one piece of minutiae after another. "We need to tell the McIvers right away. Jennie's going to be surprised," she said, opening her bedroom door. "You can get Rose or Stevetta to help you pack then Ples can load the buggy."

"I'm not packing my new bloomers. I'll be wearing them," Claire grinned.

Koi snickered. "Only pack a satchel with things you might need on the road, because there isn't room in the small buggy. Have Ples load your luggage and new purchases in the large carriage."

Koi closed the door and began to pack. She laid her calico dress on the bed to inspect it for any soiled spots. When she was satisfied it was clean, she placed it in her traveling bag. She stared off into space, reliving the past week, and felt a twinge of guilt for treating Claire so badly lately. She wondered if being with child had caused her to make mountains out of molehills. It didn't matter the reason or cause for her bad behavior. She had been wrong about Claire's intentions. Now, she would try to make it up to her.

◊◊◊

The family arrived at Ardmore later than they had planned. It was long after midnight when the two buggies pulled up in front of the hotel.

"Everyone grab your essentials and head on in. We can take care of the rest of the luggage tomorrow," John said.

Koi stepped down from the buggy, grabbed her satchel, and slung the strap over her shoulder. "We'll see y'all in the morning."

Claire grabbed hers and followed Koi along the sidewalk to the train car.

◊◊◊

Koi was wide awake when the sun came up. She lay in bed, thinking she better get out of bed and let the McIvers know she was getting married today. It took only minutes to get dressed, and she rushed out into the early morning air. She would try to be back before Claire woke up.

Koi drove Bess across town to the McIvers' house. She knocked loudly on the door and called. "Violet? Jennie?"

"Is that you, Koi?" Violet yelled.

"Yes. It's me."

Mrs. McIver opened the door, wearing a lavender robe adorned with bright purple flowers and her hair done up in paper rollers. "What brings you here so early? Come on in."

"No, thank you, Violet, I'm in a hurry. I've come to tell you

178

that Osi and I will be getting married today after the show. We're going to say our vows in the senator's train car, and I want y'all to be there. Tell Jennie she has to come. I want her to be a bridesmaid."

"She didn't bring any clothes fit for a wedding," Violet said.

"She doesn't need anything fancy. It's informal. Tell her to wear one of her calico dresses. I'll be wearing mine. Everyone else will be in their Territory clothes."

Koi stopped at the Methodist parsonage before rushing back to the train car. She was glad the preacher was there, since she needed to hire him to perform the ceremony.

By the time Koi arrived back at the depot, Claire was up, dressed, and giving orders to the porters. "Make sure you rearrange the furniture so we can accommodate all the guests." She turned and handed Koi a refreshment list. "Here, take a look at this and tell me if I forgot anything before I give it to the porters to prepare."

Koi looked at the list and smiled. "It's perfect. Thank you for being so thoughtful. I don't know how I can repay you."

"No need. We're friends, aren't we?" Claire asked.

"Of course." Koi leaned over and gave her a hug.

Claire reciprocated politely with a quick squeeze then pulled away. "We better get everything prepared before it's time for us to go."

By mid-morning, Koi and Claire had everything ready.

"I just realized we haven't had breakfast," Claire said.

"I'm so excited, I don't have an appetite," Koi replied. "Let's get to the hotel and grab something there before we go." The two talked as they walked the short distance to the hotel. "I'm eager to see how Kash is doing," Koi said as they neared the hotel. "I hope he hasn't given Gentle Woman too much trouble."

"I doubt she would complain if he did. She loves that boy."

They entered the foyer to find Gentle Woman, Kash, and Rose walking toward the door.

"What are y'all doing here in the lobby?" Koi swooped Kash up into her arms.

"We're waiting for John and Ples to bring the buggy around. Your father has already been to the campgrounds and back. He said there's a lot of people there already."

"We've been so busy preparing for the wedding we haven't had time to eat. I thought we'd get something here at the hotel and take it with us." Koi looked at Rose and noticed the big wicker picnic basket she was carrying. "What have you got in there?" Koi asked.

"Miz Koi, we's got fried chicken, corn bread, wild onions, and apricot fried pies," Rose said proudly.

"One thing for sure, we aren't going to go hungry today," Koi said.

Crowds of people were jockeying for a good place to park when the Pritchett's buggy arrived.

"There's a good spot over there," John said pointing to an open space.

Ples maneuvered the rig between two other buggies so that everyone had a clear view of the grounds.

"I see someone stacked some bales of hay on the other side of the arena for people to sit on," John observed.

"I'm glad we can just sit here in the buggy and watch. It'll be much more comfortable," Koi said.

Claire couldn't seem to sit still. "I have no idea what I'm about to see!" she exclaimed.

"You'll see all sorts of things. Trick riders, as well as roping demonstrations, bronco busting, and wild cow milking to name a few," John told her.

◇◇◇

Koi's eyes scanned the crowd, looking for Osi, but she didn't see him. She stepped from the buggy and reached for Kash. "Come, let's go see Osi." She took Kash in her arms and lifted him to the ground before turning to the others. "We'll be back in a few minutes."

Koi knew Osi would be somewhere near the holding stalls, and she quickly spotted him in back of the calf pens, checking Black Panther's hooves.

"Yoo hoo," Koi called.

Osi looked up. "Hey." He gave her a quick peck on the cheek then lifted Kash up into his arms. "Do you want to sit on Black Panther while I finish checking his hooves?"

Kash reached his arms up, trying to grab the saddle horn.

"One of these days we'll be watching him compete," Osi said.

Koi smiled proudly at the thought of Kash growing up to be like his father.

When a high-pitched whistle blew, announcing the show was about to start, Osi lifted Kash off Black Panther and handed him to Koi. "It's almost time," he said. "I'll see you afterwards."

Koi, with Kash in her arms, rushed back to her seat in the buggy.

"Did you find him?" Claire asked.

"Yes, he'll be riding in the Grand Entry shortly."

Koi barely finished her sentence when the band struck up a merry tune. Mounted riders came galloping into the arena. All eyes were drawn to Osi. He sat straight in the saddle, holding the Chickasaw flag. His long black hair, tied back, accentuated his chiseled good looks. He and Black Panther made a complete circle around the perimeter before stopping close to the rider holding the American flag. Both men remained still while the other participants entered the arena. The band stopped playing, and a moment of silence swept over the grounds before they began to play a rendition of "The Star-Spangled Banner". Everyone stood. The men wearing hats held them over their hearts. When the music stopped, the riders exited the arena while the audience clapped, hooted, and hollered.

Chapter Twenty-Four

Koi stood and scanned the area for Jennie. When she spotted the McIvers' buggy, she pointed. "There they are." When Jennie waved, Koi sat back down. "Let's go see them during intermission."

"I noticed Osi doesn't have those metal objects attached to his boots like all the others do," Claire said.

"That's because Osi doesn't need spurs with Black Panther."

John heard Koi's remark and quickly added, "Those two are keenly attuned to each other. They seem to know what the other is thinking. If you watch Osi and Black Panther closely, you'll see they move together as one." John looked at the paper in his hand. "We're supposed to be in for a big surprise today. Some cowboy from Texas is going to wrestle a bull."

A lone rider on a feisty sorrel rode back and forth from one end of the arena to the other, blowing a whistle now and then.

"What's that man with the whistle doing?" Claire asked John.

"He's the arena boss in charge of keeping the acts moving, and he'll use his timepiece to see who wins the competitive events."

The whistle blew loudly, announcing the first act. Everyone's eyes turned to a young woman, scantily clad in a white feathery outfit, ride into the arena, standing on a pair of albino ponies. She stood with one foot on each horse while they trotted around the perimeter. The crowd clapped and yelled with enthusiasm as the woman in white exited the grounds.

When the noise quieted enough to talk, John turned to

Koi. "Let's change places so I can sit next to Claire and explain what's going on."

Koi settled next to Kash and Gentle Woman just as the whistle blew, announcing the next act.

John leaned over to Claire and spoke near her ear. "The fancy rope tricks are next. They're my favorite, besides calf roping."

Two riders on horseback entered the arena from opposite ends of the field, one swinging a loop over his head. When the horses neared the center of the arena, the roper threw the twisted fibers completely over the other horse. When the rope hit the ground, the animal stepped inside the circle. With perfect timing, the roper flicked his wrist and jerked the loop taut around the horse's upper legs without causing him to fall. The crowd cheered.

John looked at his program. "He's that Cherokee from Claremore named Rogers. He's getting famous, not only his rope tricks but for his humor too. I understand he's pretty funny on stage."

Tricks with the lariats continued, with men on foot and horseback showing how they could make figures and shapes with their ropes.

"The bareback bronc riding is next. It's the most physically demanding of all the competitions because the rider has no saddle or reins for control," John told Claire.

"Does Osi ever compete in this event?"

"No. He gets enough bronc riding breaking his green horses. Some of them can be pretty rank." John smiled. "Osi's good though. He'd probably win any contest he entered, but calf roping is his specialty."

After the bronc riders had their turn, the arena boss announced the winner by raising the cowboy's hand above his head. The crowd cheered loudly.

"Does that man get any kind of prize?" Claire asked.

"Yes, sometimes it's money, and occasionally, the winner will get a saddle or belt buckle." John again looked at the paper in his hand. "The bull wrestling demonstration is next. I've heard of this Texas cowboy named Pickett, and I'm eager to see how he does it."

The whistle blew and the holding pen latch was released. A monstrous bull lunged into the arena, snorting and pawing the ground with his hooves. From the sidelines a mounted horse plunged at full speed toward the bull. When the rider reached the animal, he leaped from his saddle, turned a complete somersault along the length of the bull's back, and grabbed the bull's curved horns. With sheer strength, he twisted and thrust the fuming animal to the ground. When the wrestler finally let go of the horns, another rider waited to assist herding the bull back to the pens. The crowd roared with excitement. The man stood and raised his hands above his head.

"That man looks like a Negro!" Claire said.

"Yep. He's part Cherokee too," John answered.

When the whistle blew several times, signaling intermission, Koi stepped from the buggy and lifted Kash down. "Let's find an outhouse," she said, looking at the women in the buggy.

John pretended he didn't hear. "I think Ples and I will go have a chat with Osi."

On the way to relieve themselves, the women passed an entire cow roasting on a spit. A middle-aged woman stood at one end, slowly turning the handle to rotate the meat and keep it from burning. Juice ran from the beef. It sizzled and smoked as it hit the red hot hickory coals.

"That sure smells good. I'm hungry." Koi said.

Claire looked away. "Seeing an animal skinned and cooked like that kind of makes me squeamish, but the aroma is enticing."

"We's got fried chicken and a good picnic lunch waitin' in the buggy for us," Rose reminded them.

"I know, Rose, but if these people are selling portions, I think we should buy some on the way back."

"Let's look for some *pashofa*. Claire can't go back to Chicago before tasting our traditional food. She might like a few grape dumplings too," Gentle Woman said.

"Don't forget we'll have food waiting for us at the train car later," Claire smiled at Koi.

They found Jennie and Violet waiting in line to use the makeshift water closet.

"Jennie! I'm glad we met up. I want you to meet Claire." Koi motioned for her to come near. Jennie held out her hand and waited for Claire to respond. When she did, Jennie said, "Very nice to finally meet you. Koi's told me *many* nice things about you."

Koi looked down to her feet. She felt a sharp pain of guilt.

Jennie glanced at Koi and grinned. "This is such an exciting day. You'll finally take your vows and have your marriage recorded. This has been a long time coming."

"I can hardly believe it's happening today," Koi said.

Rose waited for a break in the conversation before she whispered to Koi, "I's be back shortly. I's gotta find an outhouse that I can use."

"That's fine, Rose. If we're not here, we'll meet you back at the buggy."

The women finally had their turn at the outdoor toilet. Violet was the last to exit. She peeked out the door to see if anyone was looking before she stepped out. "Well, that was an ordeal," she said, straightening her purple polka-dot dress with the palms of her hands.

"Jennie, we're going to sample some food before the intermission is over. Do you want to come with us?" Koi asked.

Jennie smiled. "No, thanks. We've eaten. I think we'll head back to the buggy. Matthew is watching Jacob, and he'll be needing a break. We'll see y'all later at the train car."

The starting whistle blew before Koi had time to purchase any food, and they rushed back to the buggy.

"It's about time you got back," John said. Gentle Woman shot a disgruntled look at him, which he pretended not to see. Instead, he looked down at the paper program to find the next act. "Whip cracking is next in line."

"What's whip cracking?" Claire asked.

"The men who participate in this event try to outdo each other by snapping their bull whips loudly and doing fancy tricks with 'em."

Rose came running to the buggy. "I's sorry it took me so long." She quickly took her seat. "Y'all want me to get our food out of the basket now?"

"That sounds good," Gentle Woman said.

Rose pulled out a drumstick and handed it to Kash.

"Did you take the sharp bone out first?" Koi asked.

"Yes, ma'am, I did. We don't want our boy choking on a chicken bone." Rose passed the basket to the others, letting them take what they wanted.

"There's apricot fried pies for later," Rose grinned.

◊◊◊

The whistle blew and a small girl about ten years old walked to the center of the arena. She placed a six-inch long cane stick in her mouth and turned completely around so that everyone could see it protruding from her lips. A man with a leather bullwhip looped in his hand stood about ten feet from the girl. With lightning speed he flipped the braided cowhide lash toward the girl, causing it to snap with a loud bang and at the same time cut the stick off in line with her nose without touching her. She smiled and took the remaining stub from her mouth and held it high for the audience to see. The crowd roared.

"We know a man named Amos Brooks who has a pair of oxen. He's so good with his bullwhip he can snap a fly off his animals' ears," John said.

"I have a hard time believing such a thing," Claire laughed, waving a finger at him.

John grinned. "It's true. Just ask Gentle Woman. She knows I don't exaggerate."

Several more acts followed before the calf roping grand finale was announced.

Kash had fallen asleep in Gentle Woman's lap. She gently scooted him in between her and Koi without waking him. "That boy gets heavier every day," she lamented.

The band struck up a lively march and played several bars before the first contestant was ready to start. Then the whistle blew and a rider nodded for a calf to be released. The animal shot out of the pen and ran alongside the edge of the arena before turning, allowing the roper to get a good loop around him. The calf fell, costing precious time. The roper had to wait until the calf stood before he could turn him on his side and tie his legs.

Two more participants followed, but their timing left much to be desired.

"What's wrong with those cowboys?" John asked.

Koi turned to her father. "I bet they knew they'd be up against Osi, and it threw them off."

"You're probably right. He should be next in line," John said.

All eyes looked toward the calf pens where Osi sat proudly astride Black Panther. His tight brown leather chaps hugged his thighs, making him look as if he were part of the saddle. His attention was focused solely on the moment, his eyes glued on the holding pen. He held Black Panther's reins taut, keeping him from starting too soon. The whistle sounded and Osi nodded for the gate lock to be released. The calf shot out of the pen like a bullet. Osi and Black Panther were right behind when Osi threw his looped rope, catching the animal with one graceful throw.

Black Panther immediately moved backwards, pulling the rope tight, while Osi slid from the saddle. With the tie rope in his teeth, he ran to the calf, flipped him over, secured his feet in one fell swoop, and quickly raised his hands into the air. The whistle blew and the crowd stood cheering.

"See, I told y'all he'd win," Koi said proudly.

The spectator's loud commotion woke Kash and he began to cry. Koi lifted him into her arms and gave him a big hug before handing him to Gentle Woman. "Here, take him. I'm going to see Osi." She jumped from the buggy and ran across the arena. By the time she arrived near the calf pens, Osi was surrounded by well-wishers.

Osi saw her struggling to get through the crowd and pushed his way from the opposite side until he reached her. He lifted her off the ground, swinging her round and round before setting her down. "Let's ride to the train car on Black Panther."

Koi nodded.

They rushed to Black Panther and Osi gracefully swung upwards into the saddle before reaching down to pull Koi up in front of him. She felt so tiny. His broad shoulders and thick chest dwarfed her.

Several people gasped at the sight of a woman riding astride. Koi didn't care what they thought. She was with the man she loved and nothing else mattered. She smiled and gave the crowd a friendly wave when Osi let Black Panther have his head.

Chapter Twenty-Five

Black Panther ran at full speed until he reached the hotel stable. Osi slid from the saddle, lifted Koi down, and handed the reins to the livery attendant. "He needs a good rub down. I've been pushing him pretty hard today."

Koi brushed the dust off her dress. "I wondered where we were going."

Osi smiled. "I have a surprise for you." He took her hand and led her inside the hotel. He guided her up a flight of stairs, pulled a room key from his watch pocket, and opened the door to the bridal suite. Koi stared at the luxurious furnishings without moving. Osi swept her up into his arms and carried her inside.

His masculine scent of sweat, leather, and cow manure was familiar to Koi and she loved it. She kissed his salty neck before he playfully threw her on the bed.

"I hope you like our quarters for the night," Osi laughed.

Koi scooted off the bed and stood before him. "I'm surprised and thrilled. It's comforting to know we'll come here after the wedding. I was beginning to wonder if we were going to have to sleep in the train car with Claire."

Osi raised an eyebrow. "I'd have said no to that. I'll be glad when she leaves."

"Me too," Koi agreed.

Osi walked to a marble washstand and began to clean up while Koi inspected the room. She hadn't stayed in a room this luxurious since her father had rented a suite for them while they were in Chicago. Curiosity caused her to look inside the tall wooden chifferobe and open any drawers she could find. She noticed a small door across the room. She opened it to find a water closet with a shower. "Look, Osi. We can wash up in here."

Osi stood shirtless in front of the washbasin, his long hair falling on his shoulders. He stepped away with his wet face dripping. "Well, I'll be. I didn't see that when I reserved the room." He unbuckled his chaps and pants, letting them drop to the floor before stepping inside.

Koi's heart skipped a beat knowing by the end of the day she would legally be Mrs. Jordan "Osi" Nance. She didn't know when she would tell him about the new baby, but she knew it would have to be soon.

She picked up Osi's chaps and pants from the floor then retrieved his shirt from a chair, shaking the dust off before hanging them in the wardrobe. Next she removed her calico dress and undergarments. She stood naked, looking at her clothes and wondering what she would do if they were dirty. She wished she hadn't worn them to the wild west show, but she had, and now she was going to have to put them back on for the ceremony.

"Koi?" Osi yelled. "I forgot to get something to dry off with."

Koi remembered seeing cotton cloths in a chest of drawers. "I'll hand you a towel." She opened the shower door and thrust it inside.

Osi grabbed her by the arm and pulled her into the shower stall with him. He drew her close as beads of falling water covered their bodies from head to toe, reminding Koi of their special place on Pennington Creek. They were both lost in a moment of bliss and in no hurry to get to the train car.

◊◊◊

Koi was dressed in her red calico when she pulled the curtain away from the south window that faced the train depot. She saw her father's buggy parked next to the McIvers'. "Oh, my goodness, we're going to be late for our own wedding."

"They can't start without us," Osi said, buckling his belt. "Let's go and get this over with."

Together they walked the short distance to the senator's

train car. As they neared the platform, Koi said, "Claire's even had the exterior decorated. Look at all those white streamers."

When they reached the door, Claire swung it open. "It's about time you arrived. Come in." When they stepped inside, they were immediately swamped by friends and family.

Koi's eyes scanned the room for Kash. He and Jacob were in a corner, playing with alphabet blocks. She smiled, knowing he was well taken care of and having a good time.

Claire rang the bell near the door to quiet the guests and raised her voice. "We're ready to start, please have a seat." Closing the door, she reached for something on a side table. Koi, still standing nearby, looked to see what she was doing. "These are for you," Claire said. She handed Koi an orange blossom bouquet and placed a matching wreath on her head. "These flowers are supposed to bring the wearer a life of happiness and an abundance of children."

Koi smiled, leaned over, and gave her a peck on the cheek. "Thank you. These are lovely. I have no idea where you purchased these blossoms this time of year."

Claire winked and whispered, "They're made of wax."

Koi raised her eyebrows and looked down the aisle to see the minister standing at the opposite end. She and Claire had discussed the order in which the ceremony would be performed, but she had forgotten to tell Osi. She leaned over and whispered in his ear, "Just do what I do."

Osi nodded.

Koi looked at the seated guests and noticed that two important people were missing. "Where's Ples and Rose?" she asked.

"They're waiting outside. It's pretty crowded in here," Claire said.

"They're family to me, so we're going to have to make room for them."

Without another word being said, Osi slipped out the door and came back shortly with Ples and Rose. When they entered, Gentle Woman motioned for Rose to come share her chair. Ples was offered a seat, but he refused to sit down. He continued to stand at the back of the room.

When everyone had settled, Koi nodded to Claire that

she was ready to start."

"As you know, we don't have room in here for a piano or a band, so the next best thing is a music box." Claire moved to an ornately engraved silver case. She opened the lid and "Beautiful Dreamer" began to play.

Koi wondered if Claire knew that was Osi's favorite song, or if it was sheer coincidence she chose that tune. It didn't matter. She was glad.

The wedding couple kept time with the music as they walked to the minister. He began the ceremony like all others, but when he came to the part about giving the bride to the groom, he skipped over it and continued. Koi had made it clear to him that she didn't want to be given away and she didn't want vows to obey. When he eliminated the words Koi didn't want, there wasn't much left to be said. The preacher looked at Osi, "Repeat after me. With this ring, I thee wed."

Osi repeated the words, pulled a simple gold band from his watch pocket, and slipped it onto Koi's ring finger.

"I now pronounce you man and wife. You may kiss the bride."

They kissed and turned to face the guests. Everyone stood, clapped, and began wishing the couple a long and happy marriage.

Claire's voice rose above the noise. "Refreshments are on the way!" She went to Koi and hugged her. "I'm so happy for you." Then she turned to Osi, threw her arms around his neck, and planted a longer than normal, passionate kiss on his lips. Not expecting her to be so bold, he stepped back.

For the first time since Claire had arrived, Koi felt no jealousy. She had accepted her as a friend with all her flirty faults. Nevertheless, she inched close to Osi and hugged his arm. "That's enough of that," she joked.

Porters carrying large trays of food and drink arrived. The first platter held long-stemmed crystal glasses filled with purple grape juice. When all the guests had been served, Claire held her glass high above her head. "Here's a toast to the happiest couple I know." She clinked her glass against the bridal couple's then lifted it to her lips. The rest of the guests followed. Congratulatory remarks continued while the porters passed trays of food.

Michael McIver turned to his wife. "Too bad the Territory is dry, otherwise, we'd be drinking champagne."

Violet slapped him on the knee and lifted her peacock feather fan to cover the blush on her face. "Keep your voice down. Someone might hear you."

Jennie inched her way to Koi. "I'm so happy. We've both waited a long time for this day, but I thought you were going to have me and Claire as your bridesmaids."

"I'm sorry, Jennie. That was my intention, but as you can see, there's barely room to move in here. I hope you aren't offended."

"Of course not. I'm just glad you did it," Jennie said, giving her a hug.

The party continued until the children became restless and began to cry. Gentle Woman and Violet tried to no avail to comfort their grandsons. Finally, Gentle Woman said, "I think it's time to take Kash and put him to bed. We have a long trip ahead of us tomorrow."

"It's time for us to go too," Violet replied. "Matthew and Jennie are going back to Tishomingo in the morning."

"When are you and Michael going to move to Tish'?" Gentle Woman asked.

"If I had my way, it couldn't be soon enough. I miss this boy." Violet kissed Jacob's chubby brown cheek.

When Koi saw Gentle Woman preparing to leave, she went to her. "You'll probably be gone before we leave in the morning, because we plan to stay and see Claire off."

Koi kissed Kash on the head then turned to Rose and gave her a hug. "I'm so glad you were here."

"Miz Koi, I's glad you wanted me."

Claire tapped her crystal glass with a silver utensil. "I need everyone's attention. There are small baskets under the chairs, filled with rose petals to throw when Koi and Osi leave. I also have a surprise for them. As you know, it would be customary to have a horse-drawn carriage take them to their honeymoon suite, but since the hotel is only a couple blocks away, I've arranged for the porters to give them a ride on a pushcart."

Koi and Osi giggled when they saw the decorated luggage carrier at the bottom of the platform. White silk streamers waved in the breeze. Every visible piece of wood had been covered with the billowy cloth. Red roses adorned the makeshift carriage.

"This is a wedding none of us will ever forget," Osi said. He took Koi's hand and helped her onto the cart before taking a seat beside her. Two uniformed porters pushed the vehicle while the guests plummeted the bride and groom with rose petals.

◊◊◊

That night Koi lay naked in bed, waiting for Osi to finish cleaning up. Finally, he stepped out of the water closet, lifted the bedcovers, and slipped in next to her. He snuggled up close and gave her a quick kiss.

"I don't know about you, but I am exhausted." Osi's head had no sooner hit the pillow than he was sound asleep.

Koi stared at the ceiling, knowing she would have to wait for another time to tell him about the baby.

◊◊◊

The next morning Koi and Osi ate breakfast with Claire in the train car.

"We want to thank you for being so generous. Our wedding was a most unusual one. I'm sure none of our guests will ever forget," Koi said.

"It was my pleasure. I'm hoping you'll be coming to Chicago to attend Eli's and my wedding in June."

"We'll try." Koi looked at Osi. He nodded and continued to puff on his cigar. Koi knew the baby would probably put a damper on traveling, but she wasn't ready to mention it.

There was a sudden jolt and the Pullman car moved. "That must be the switchmen hooking us up to the train," Claire said.

"Then that's our signal to go," Osi replied.

Claire walked them to the platform and bid them goodbye. "Please write, and hopefully, we'll see you this spring in Chicago."

The train began to slowly move away from the Ardmore depot, headed northbound to Chicago. Claire stood on the car platform, waving until the train was out of site.

◊◊◊

Koi ordered a box lunch from the hotel restaurant while Osi retrieved Black Panther, Bess, and the small buggy from the livery stable. He placed his saddle in the buggy and tied Black Panther's reins to the back. Then he climbed into the driver's seat with Koi beside him. They were soon on their way to Tishomingo.

When the buggy crossed Pennington Creek Bridge, Osi turned to Koi. "I want to take a little detour before we go home."

As they passed through town and onto a familiar road, Koi asked, "Are we going to Lookout Mound?"

"Yes. It's been a long time since we've been there."

Osi pulled Bess to a stop on top of the tall mound and helped Koi down. They stood knee deep in dried wildflowers. A hint of fall was in the air.

"The last time we were here, my hat blew off and you had to run after it," Koi said.

"Yes, and I remember telling you that *someday* I'd build a house for us on this very spot." Osi took the lap robe from the buggy seat, spread it on the ground, and pulled Koi onto the blanket with him. They lay on their backs, looking at the puffy whipped cream clouds.

"That *someday* is getting close," Osi said.

Koi cupped Osi's face and looked him in the eye. "I hope it won't be too long, because our family is expanding. Kash will have a little brother or sister, come spring."

"Are you teasing me?"

Koi smiled. "No. It's true. We're going to have a baby."

Osi pulled her close to his chest. "I love you more than anything," he whispered. He continued to cradle her in his arms

195

as he prayed silently to Ababinnili, giving thanks for all his many blessings, before saying, "I guess for now we better get home to Okla Chuka."

BOOKS
by
Mary Ruth Hughes

Native American:

TISHOMINGO
RETURN TO OKLA CHUKA
WILLOW FLOWER'S GIFT
NATIVE AMERICAN RECIPES

Children's Whimsical Halloween:

THE OLD TOAD
JUNK FOOD MUMMY
GHOST DANCIN' ZYDECO
MONSTERS
CREATURES
MONSTER BALL

Memoir:

MEMORIES OF A FARMER'S DAUGHTER
by
Jennie Phelps

All books available at:
Amazon.com
barnesandnoble.com
MaryRuthHughes.com
Kindle
Gift shops throughout the United States

Made in the USA
Charleston, SC
28 July 2016